PERFECT ENEMY

WALL STREET JOURNAL & USA TODAY BESTSELLING AUTHOR

M. ROBINSON

PERFECT ENEMY

M. ROBINSON

© 2023 Perfect Enemy by M. Robinson

DEDICATION

*To readers who love the anti-hero with
a dirty mouth and big cock.*

AUTHOR'S NOTE

For Content Warnings, please visit my website:

www.authormrobinson.com

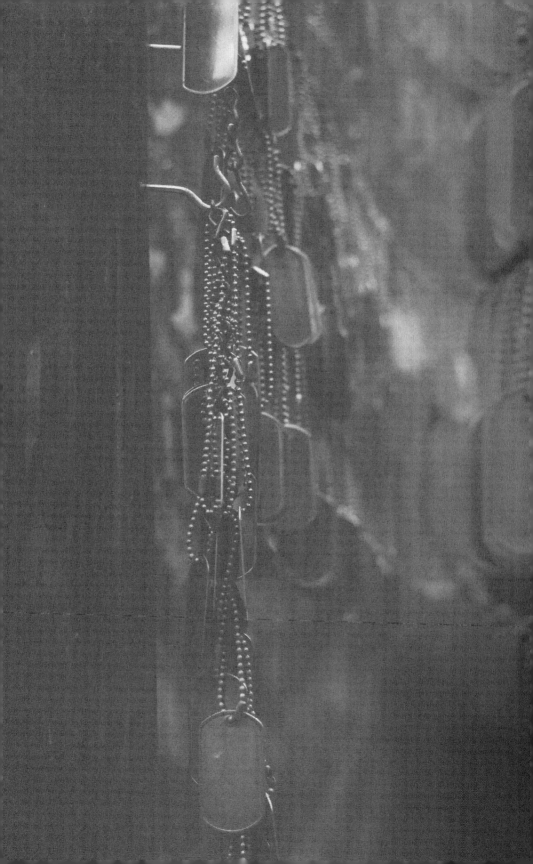

PROLOGUE

JACE

I watched with stone-cold eyes as the shiny black casket was lowered into the dirt ground, taking my mother's body with it. Heaven cried right along with my family as raindrops seeped into my crisp white Navy SEAL dress uniform. With each drop, I felt a little more of myself die along with her until darkness surrounded me despite it being broad daylight.

I could feel everyone's eyes on me like a noose around my neck. Especially my family's. They were waiting for me to react, waiting for me to break down, waiting for me to do something.

Anything.

Trust me, I wanted to comfort my family…

I just didn't know how anymore.

I was twenty-eight years old and should have been the son who'd spent the most time with her, but I had been defending my country for the past ten years. I enlisted the day I graduated from high school. The Navy made me a man even though I felt like a little boy who simply yearned for his mother's love at that moment.

I was Elite Forces—the best of the best by land, sea, and air. I led missions, did offensive raids, demolitions, reconnaissance, search and rescue, and counterterrorism. There wasn't anything I couldn't do. I made sure of it. My career was my life, and sadly enough, I wasn't around for my family. I was the eldest of six kids in the Beckham household, with a twenty-year age gap between me and my youngest sibling, Haven.

She was only eight years old, and her whole world was crashing down on her. I didn't know how to comfort any of them. I remained the hardened soldier I was trained to be; desensitizing myself was how I stayed on top.

I internalized all of my emotions; burying them deep inside me was the only way I'd survive this day and the future.

I didn't get to say goodbye to her.

I missed so many holidays, birthdays, and special events. The list was endless of how much time I lost with her. The guilt was eating me alive. I felt like I couldn't breathe, as if I stopped breathing right along with her.

One fatal car accident changed our entire lives by a fucking fifteen-year-old punk-ass kid who was selling drugs. All I wanted was one minute alone with him. He should have been the one who was buried that morning, not our mother.

I couldn't tell you how long I stood there watching my life unravel in front of my eyes. It could have been a minute, an hour, or a day that flew by. Time just seemed to stand still while everything shattered around me.

Piece by piece.

One by one.

After today, nothing would be left of me.

Suddenly, I felt Haven's hand in my grasp, and I glanced down to look at her. Her eyes were swollen, her cheeks were sunken, and her face was pale. She looked like she had aged ten years overnight. She was no longer the little girl my parents prayed for. After twenty years and five sons, their prayers were finally answered. Haven had the least amount of time with her, and now she'd be surrounded by only men as she grew up and became a woman.

I wouldn't be there to watch it happen. My duty was to my country, and I'd return to the battlefield with a broken heart and a guilty conscience. I thought I had all the time in the world to be part of my family. Instead, I just lost the biggest part of what made us one.

Tears loosely flowed down Haven's face, breaking my heart a little more if that was even possible. I wanted to hug her, kiss her, tell her everything would be all right.

I didn't.

I couldn't.

It'd be a lie.

And I was a lot of things, but I wasn't a liar.

While I held one of her hands, her best friend, Cove, held the other, offering her support the only way an eight-year-old could. I once again brought my stare forward, squeezing Haven's tiny grasp and providing the only comfort I knew how to give. I thought about how much she looked like our mother. You'd think I'd find solace in that. Instead, it was pure and utter torture.

My brother Reid, their second son, gave the eulogy. I was the soldier, and still, I couldn't bring myself to do it. I tried to stay present, but it was no use. I was lost in my own hell, waiting for I don't know what to occur because my nightmare had only just begun.

I didn't get to say goodbye to her.

It echoed in my mind like a broken record.

It was the only thing I heard…

Felt.

It completely consumed me.

Deeper and deeper, I sought refuge within me, fully aware nothing would ever be the same again.

Especially our family.

When the funeral was over, everyone in attendance returned to our house with food, drinks, and condolences. I swear if one more person told me how sorry they were, I would lose my shit. From the second I stepped inside the front door, it no longer felt like home. The woman who made it one was gone forever.

Except I kept seeing her everywhere.

There was no escaping her memory. It was engraved in the walls—she was in every corner, every crevice. Her presence was everywhere and all at once. From the floor to the ceiling to the decorations to the happiness she brought into our lives with just a smile or a few words of reassurance. What I'd give to tell her I loved her just one last time and feel like her little boy.

"I'm so sorry, Jace. Please know—"

I nodded, cutting off my father's secretary who helped him run the ranch in our town of Jackson Hole, Wyoming. Everyone knew who we were, and a line of people waited around our house to give their condolences, but all I wanted was to slam the door right in their faces.

Before I knew what I was doing, I started drinking, thinking it would make it easier on me. It didn't. If anything, it made it harder. The moment I realized I was drinking myself into an utter blackout rage, I grabbed the bottle of Jack and left my childhood home through the kitchen door.

Never once looking back.

I was a grenade ready to fucking explode if I didn't get the hell out of there, which was the last thing anybody needed.

Including *me*.

COVE

"Do you need another hug, Haven?"

My best friend shook her head with her eyes still glued to the floor in her living room.

I hated that this was happening, and I couldn't do anything for her and her family. What I really hated was that I didn't understand why it was happening to them in the first place. This was all so confusing, and nobody would explain it to me.

Why do people have to die?

Mrs. Beckham was the best, and I missed her so much already. She always made me feel like I was part of their family, and now I was scared I wouldn't have one anymore. My parents didn't want me. They were never around. I always had a nanny, but they changed all the time.

Maybe it was me? Was I unlovable? Was something wrong with me?

Haven and I became best friends four years ago in preschool. Since then, Mrs. Beckham was the only mom I'd ever known. Now she was gone forever, and all I wanted was for someone to tell me why she had to die.

Was she in heaven? Would I ever see her again?

Her brothers were quiet, and her dad was really sad. Today was the first time I'd seen their daddy cry, and it hurt my heart so much. It felt like it was breaking inside me, and I hated not being able to do anything about it.

I only felt a little better today when I saw Jace walk into the church. He wore his white Navy uniform and looked like Prince Eric from *The Little Mermaid*. Except he wasn't smiling like he usually was. His smiles were always my favorite thing about him.

He wasn't around a lot, but every time he was, my stomach would bubble, and my heart would go super fast. He was the best big brother to Haven, and when he was in town, he'd hang out with us. Of course, I'd pretend it wasn't a big deal, but it was a huge one.

Haven didn't know I liked her brother. I thought my crush would just go away, but every time I saw him, it only made my feelings worse. I felt like the worst best friend on the planet for keeping this secret from her. We always told each other everything. I was scared she'd be mad at me for having a crush on him. Best friends weren't supposed to like each other's brothers.

Those were the rules, right?

Since I was trying to make Jace feel better, I asked my nanny if she'd help me make his favorite red velvet cake. I brought it over for the family, but I saved the last piece for him.

When I saw him leave through the kitchen door, I couldn't help myself.

"Haven, I'll be right back, okay?"

She nodded, still not looking at me.

I hurried toward my backpack and grabbed the piece of cake I saved for him. I also took my favorite stuffed animal with me—a bunny I won at the arcade when I was six. It always made me feel better when I missed my parents and felt alone at night.

Before he was out of sight, I quickly rushed out the kitchen door behind him, worried I wouldn't be able to find him. I was lucky to catch him walking into the woods at the last second. It was almost dark out. I wasn't supposed to go outside by myself when the sun went down, but since I'd be with him, and he was grown up, I didn't think I'd get in trouble.

I followed him without making a peep until he stopped in front of what looked like a river deep in the woods behind their house. I never knew it was even back there. It was so pretty and quiet. It reminded me of my *River and Streams* book, one of my favorites to read to myself.

Jace was staring out at the water for what felt like forever until he finally asked, "What do you want, Cove?"

His question surprised me. "How did you know I was here?"

"I'm trained to."

"You could feel me like a superhero does?"

He turned to face me. "Something like that."

Only then did I see how different he looked from what I was used to. His hair was a mess, and his eyes were bright red and super glossy. It didn't look like he'd been crying, but the strong smell of liquor blew in my face. He was holding a bottle of what I heard my dad call whiskey. Sometimes he'd act funny if he had too many glasses.

I smiled a little, stepping toward Jace to let him know I was only there to try to make him feel better. Once I stood in front of him, I tried handing him my piece of cake and stuffed animal.

"I made your favorite cake for you. It's red velvet, and this is my bunny. It always makes me feel better, so you can borrow it for as long as you want. You can keep it too. It's my present for you."

I never expected what happened next.

I thought… I don't know what I thought, but what he did hurt me in ways I never thought he would.

He took one look at my gifts before smacking them right out of my hands, making me gasp loudly.

"Jace—"

In a mean voice, he snapped, "What are you doing here, Cove? You're not even family."

7

I jerked back, frowning.

"You're always here. Always around. You're not my parents' responsibility."

"I'm sorry, Jace." I could feel the tears in my eyes. "I was just trying to help make you feel better. I didn't mean to make you mad at me."

"Make me feel better?" he taunted.

"I'm… I'm… I was just… I mean… I'm sorry your mom died."

I saw it clear as day. His bright-blue eyes turned dark like he was suddenly the villain in one of my Disney movies.

"What you should be sorry for," he scolded, "is following me out here and not minding your own damn business."

"Why are you being so mean to me?"

"You think this is mean? You have no idea what I'm capable of. The things I've seen and done…" He shook his head for a second, almost like he remembered something he didn't want to. "What you need to do is turn your ass around and go waste someone else's time. I don't need anything from you, Cove. Do you understand me?"

I couldn't help it. I burst into tears, running back up to their house. I didn't want him to see me cry.

Because the truth was, Jace Beckham wasn't just my first real crush. He was also the first guy…

To break my heart completely.

CHAPER 1
COVE
NOW: 10 YEARS LATER

"Cove, have you seen my purse?" Mom asked, walking into the kitchen.

"I think it's by the door."

"Honey, you need some makeup. You're looking pale."

I sighed. "Gee, thanks, Mom. Nice to see you too."

"What's with the attitude?"

"No attitude. I just haven't seen you in two weeks, and the first thing you say is how shitty I look."

"Don't cuss. It's not ladylike, and I didn't use the word shitty."

"Right…"

"Darling, would you rather I lie to you? You're not going to be homecoming queen looking pale. Now, are you?"

"I have no desire to be homecoming queen, and you'd know that if you were involved in my life."

"I was homecoming queen, and so was your grandmother and great-grandmother. It's practically a tradition. You wouldn't want to disappoint me, would you?"

The sad thing was, I didn't. I kept thinking if I checked off all her boxes, she'd eventually love me in the way I needed her to. In the way I needed them *both* to. It was a dumb and naive assumption, but it didn't take away the desire to please them.

"How dare if I did, right?"

"Don't take that tone with me, young lady. You've had everything you've ever wanted. I would have killed to have a mother like me. You should be grateful we've always treated you like an adult and not a child."

"Except when I was actually a child," I mumbled under my breath.

"Now be a doll and go put on some blush. I refuse to have a daughter who doesn't look her best at all times. How do you think I've kept your father happy all these years? Beautiful women get far in life, Cove."

"Yeah, so do smart ones."

"You don't need to be smart, sweetheart. You just need to marry a man who is. And let's face it, you're not the brightest crayon in the box."

"Mom, I have a 3.9 cumulative GPA, and every college I've applied to has offered me a full scholarship."

She shut the fridge, not paying me any mind. "Hmm… that's nice, honey."

She wasn't even listening to me. She never did. Most of the time, it seemed as if I was a burden to both of them rather than their daughter. However, she wasn't lying. They always gave me everything I ever wanted except for their love and attention. The older I got, the worse it seemed to get.

Now that I was eighteen and an adult, there was no reason for them to parent me, but the reality was, they never did. Various nannies and housekeepers raised me, but mostly, I raised myself. I spent more time at Haven's house than at my own. She was the only family I had, and with the loss of her mother, we relied on each other.

"We'll be back next week," Mom stated, smiling wide. "Your father is accepting an award for surgeon of the year in Miami. We decided to make a family vacation out of it."

"Family vacation, huh?"

"Cove, don't frown. It causes wrinkles."

I simply nodded.

"Oh, I know! We'll bring you back a gift. How does a Prada bag sound?"

"Great, I'll add it to the dozens of Prada bags you've brought me home. Maybe I can be included on the family trip next time?"

"Honey"—she giggled—"you don't want to hang out with your parents when you could be hanging out with all your friends. You're one of the most popular girls in your school. What you need to be focusing your time on is finding a boyfriend at an Ivy League university before your beauty starts fading. You won't be young forever, Cove."

"For fuck's sake," I whispered to myself.

She kissed the air. "Be a good girl while we're gone, okay?"

I simply nodded. It was easier to deal with her when I just agreed with everything she said. I was once again left to fend for myself. You'd think I'd be used to it, considering they neglected me my whole life. I was only useful to them when they needed to show me off to their friends or at their parties. I was nothing more than a toy they could play with whenever they wanted.

I'd be graduating in a few short months and moving out. I couldn't help but fear the reality that I'd truly be alone.

Would they have me over for holidays? Would they even notice I was gone and wasn't living there with them?

My cell phone rang with Haven's picture on the screen. I answered, but she sounded panicked before I could say hello, announcing, "I need you."

I was immediately worried. "What's wrong?"

"So much. Can you meet me at my house?"

"I'm on my way."

As I was driving, I had a sneaking suspicion it had something to do with Hayes, the guy she was hopelessly falling for. I'd only seen him a few times, but it was obvious my best friend was falling in love for the first time. To complicate matters, he was her boss at the bar where she waitressed.

We didn't live far from one another. It didn't take me long to arrive on their property. Since there were no cars, I assumed no one was home. I waited for her in my Jeep in her driveway. I was surprised I didn't see her brothers' vehicles. Haven's house had always been a revolving door for her five older siblings. She was the only one who still technically lived at home, but you wouldn't think that with how often they were there.

Each one was a pain in the ass in their own way, though none of them held a candle to Jace. Now that he was retired from the Navy, he was at their house more than I cared for. The last thing I wanted was to run into him without her being home.

I couldn't stand the asshole. He was worse than ever when it came to her. They all treated Haven like she was still a little girl despite her being eighteen and graduating from high school soon. They didn't give a shit.

It seemed as if Jace was trying to make up for lost time. The Navy had always been his life, and I only saw him a couple of times a year in the last decade. Thank God for that. Just thinking about him pissed me off.

From the moment he treated me like shit when I was eight years old,

I kept my distance from him. We barely spoke to one another, and when we did, it was filled with animosity and hatred. I never knew why he hated me. All I knew was that I despised him.

"Haven, where are you?" I rasped to myself while grabbing the pack of cigarettes from my purse.

Between her guy drama and my parents' absence, I was feeling anxious. Haven hated that I sometimes smoked, but it helped take the edge off. Out of the two of us, my best friend was definitely the angel, and I was the devil on her shoulder.

If her brothers truly knew the things I'd made her do over the years, they'd never let her leave their house. She was hiding her relationship or whatever Hayes and her were to one another from her family. It was the only way she'd be able to have him in her life, and we both knew it.

I, for one, was proud of her for finally standing her ground on something she wanted. I never understood how she'd let them control her like they did. However, sometimes I was jealous of how much they loved her. For years, I wished I had that.

I thought being popular would fill the void in my heart. When that didn't work, I started hanging out with guys, hoping to fall in love with one of them or find someone who loved me. It was the opposite; men simply wanted one thing from me, and I refused to give it to someone who wasn't worthy of my body.

It didn't mean I wasn't a flirt or loved the attention I received on the daily. I used it to my advantage, hoping to meet my soulmate eventually.

I shook off the sentiment, rolling down the window and lighting a cigarette. I only smoked when I felt this way because it helped calm me down. Bringing the cigarette up to my lips, I inhaled deeply. Out of nowhere, it was roughly ripped out of my hand, causing me to snap around.

I came face-to-face with the person I least expected.

Jace fucking Beckham.

The bane of my existence.

"What the fu—"

"Do I need to remind you that smoking causes cancer?"

My eyes widened, instantly furious as I watched him throw the cigarette to the ground and stub it out with his boot.

Meeting my glare, he questioned, "When the hell did you pick up this bad habit?"

I couldn't believe the balls on this man.

With a shrug, I sassed, "Probably around the same time I started smoking crack and spreading my legs for truck drivers at rest stops."

"Cove…"

"Jace…" I mocked in the same snide tone he was using on me.

"I won't ask you again."

"Lovely. Then I won't have to repeat myself." I pulled out another cigarette, but he yanked the pack out of my hand.

"Jace!" I stormed out of my Jeep, getting in his face. "Give it back! Now!"

He held it away from me.

"I mean it." I reached for the pack again. "Give them to me!"

"Not a chance in hell."

"Jesus!" This was the first time he played this parental card on me. "What's your problem?"

"Currently," he declared, "you are."

"Who the hell do you think *you are?* You can't boss me around like you do your sister."

"Well, someone has to."

"Oh my God!" I lunged for the pack, but he gripped my throat and shoved my back against my Jeep door.

I tried to yank his hand away, but his hold was too firm, so I held his wrist instead.

"You got a death wish, Cove?"

Scowling, I demanded, "Let go of me."

"No."

"You have no right to do this to me."

"From where I'm standing, I have all the right in the world to protect Haven from your rebellious teenage bullshit."

"I'm eighteen, asshole. You know I'm an adult."

"I know you think you are."

"I don't need your approval on what I can and can't do, G.I. Joe. Haven doesn't smoke. Okay? It's a me thing."

He eyed me up and down before slowly letting go of me and backing away.

I reached for the pack again, thinking he would hand it back to me. Except he didn't. In one quick motion, he threw the pack on the ground and roughly stepped on them with the heel of his boot.

I gasped, caught off guard.

"If I catch you smoking again," he warned in a voice I didn't appreciate, "we're going to have a problem. And trust me, Cove."

Without any hesitation, he added...

"You don't want to fuck with me."

CHAPTER 2
COVE

As soon as I saw Haven pull in, I jumped out of my car and darted toward hers. She was crying when I opened her door.

"Oh my God! What's going on?"

"Oh, Cove..."

She immediately threw her arms around my neck, breaking down.

"Haven." I rubbed her back. "You're freaking me out. What happened?"

Once she calmed down and we were in her bedroom, she finally shared some unsettling news about why she was so upset. I felt the weight of her words and tried to listen before I gave my opinion on the fucked-up situation she found herself in.

"He's been warning me for months he is not who I think he is, and now I'm like, why didn't I believe him?"

Hayes was the bad boy her brothers would destroy if they found out she was dating.

After we went back and forth for a minute, I replied with the only thing that seemed right. "The way I see it, he's got a darker side to him." I continued, doing my best to reassure her.

"That's what scares me. What if he does this all the time?"

"Maybe he just takes out bad guys."

"This isn't *Dexter*, Cove."

I smirked. "I love that show."

To me, Haven hit the jackpot with Hayes. I'd love to have a man who was fearless and a badass.

She shook her head. "We are not the same. How are we best friends?"

"Opposites attract. What's your next move?"

"I don't know."

"How did the fight end?"

"With him telling me to stay away from him. He said it was the only way he could protect me."

"Is that what you want to do?"

"Of course I want to be with him, but not in that life."

"Your brothers would flip their shit."

"I know. Could you imagine?"

"I don't want to imagine it."

It was too hard to envision them ever letting her grow up, and by the sound of the rest of our conversation, she knew it too.

"I wish I could just ask and get a straight answer from him," she added. "I know nothing about him, Cove. He doesn't share anything with me other than how bad he is for me."

"Maybe there's a reason for that too."

"Ugh! I hate it when you make sense."

I smiled. "I'm wise beyond my years."

"You are."

I had to ask, "Do you think he has any single friends?"

"Oh my God! You're horrible."

"What?" I shrugged again. "You may find what he does scary, but I'm digging it. I'd love a man who wouldn't think twice about laying someone out if it meant I was safe. That shit would make me spread my legs like no tomorrow," I honestly spoke.

"Cove!"

"I'm just saying, I want a badass too. Especially if he has a big dick. That's very important as well."

"Says the girl who's still a virgin."

"Umm…" I gestured to myself, once again speaking the truth. "Do you see this temple that I am? I won't just give it to someone who takes me out to a nice restaurant a few times. High school guys are boring, Haven. College men are even worse. They're all into themselves, and I want someone who's only into me."

"Are you saying you want an older guy? Hayes is seven years older than me."

"Mmm…" I thought about it for a second. "I don't think I'd go over like twentyish."

"Twenty?! That could be your dad."

"My dad didn't have me until he was in his thirties."

My father only had me because my mother wanted another accessory she could show off to validate her self-worth.

"Well, it could be somebody's dad."

"No." I shook my head. "I definitely don't want any baby mama drama. It needs to be someone with no strings attached to an ex."

"Yeah, but then you get a man like Jace who's worked his entire life."

I glared at her. "Don't ever say that again. You just ruined my entire fantasy."

"My brother's not so bad."

"On what scale? He's worse than ever now that he's retired military. It's like he has this permanent stick up his ass. I don't remember the last time I saw him smile. He's always so broody and grumpy. Your brother needs to get laid. I bet it's been years for him."

"Ew."

"My thoughts exactly."

She smiled. "I wouldn't mind you marrying one of my brothers. Then we could be real sisters."

"Trust me, Haven. Out of all your brothers, Jace would be the last one I'd ever marry. I'd rather die single and lonely than spend five minutes alone with that asshole. He's like my perfect enemy."

I hated him in ways I never thought I could hate anyone. He was the absolute worst. Hearing Haven speak so nonchalantly about me marrying one of her brothers wasn't exactly a shock. We'd love to be sisters, but I'd never in a million years consider being with Jace Beckham.

Fuck him and the horse he rode in on.

She opened her mouth to reply, but there was a knock on her door.

"Come in," she hollered.

The door opened, revealing her brother Reid.

"Hey," he greeted, smiling at us with that charismatic expression.

Reid was the CEO of a commercial property development enterprise that he started when he was twenty-one. The family threw him a big party to celebrate the day he applied for his LLC. Their father was always involved in each of their lives. Mr. Beckham stepped into the role of both parents as if he'd prepared for it all his life.

Reid was thirty-three and fucking loaded, traveling all over the world. He worked twenty-four seven, and every year like clockwork, *Forbes* magazine labeled him one of their most eligible bachelors. The press loved Reid. He was charming and loved the attention. Like all of Haven's brothers, women flocked to him.

The Beckham boys were handsome, and women just itched to get a taste of them. It'd been that way our entire lives, driving Haven crazy that the same rules for her didn't apply to them.

"Hey," Reid interrupted my thoughts. "You listening to me?"

Haven shook her head. "Yeah, sorry, what was that?"

"I said we're all going to the pool hall. You two want to come?"

"Umm…"

I answered for her. "We'd love to. We'll be down in a minute."

"All right, don't take forever."

Once he was gone, she chastised me. "What the hell? You think I want to go out right now?"

"No, and that's all the more reason to. Listen, I'll sit up here with you all night if that's what you want to do, but I think it'd be good for you to go out and spend some time with your brothers. You haven't been around that much. They're going to start getting suspicious. Plus, it'd be good for you to be around family. It's your favorite thing in the world."

"My boyfriend may have killed someone, and you think the solution is to go play pool?"

"There's dancing too."

"Cove…"

"Have I ever steered you wrong?"

"Yes."

I laughed. "If it weren't for me, you'd be a nun."

"I basically already am. Hayes won't touch me, remember?"

"Haven." I sighed deeply. "It's time you learn that your pussy holds all the power. If you want him to touch it, then give him a reason to."

My best friend did not understand men. Thank God she had me to steer her in the right direction or who knows what'd come of her future.

From the moment we walked into the pool hall, the place was packed to the brim with people. Luckily, we found an empty table near the back. It was the first time we were out with all her brothers in what felt like forever. I couldn't remember the last time they were together like this, and I knew Haven would thank me for making her come out with them.

After we ordered food, Jace questioned her. "You okay?"

He was always so perceptive—it was so fucking annoying.

"Yeah." Haven nodded. "I'm just tired."

Jace proceeded to ride her ass, making me roll my eyes.

Unable to help myself, I asked, "Why are we picking on Haven?" Bringing their attention over to me, I stated, "She's eighteen now. She's allowed to have a life. You all did."

I was over the fact they thought they could continue to control every second of her life. It was bullshit. None of them had someone breathing down their necks twenty-four seven. They could all make their own decisions, and their sister deserved the same respect.

"It doesn't matter how old she is." Jace nodded at her. "She's our little sister."

"Except she's not so little anymore."

"All righty..." Haven interrupted. She was aware this could escalate quickly.

Jace could push my buttons as if he knew every last one.

"So on that note," she informed, "I'm going to go to the bathroom. I'll be right back."

After she left, it was fair game.

"If you keep hounding her like you do, Jace, she'll end up pushing you away."

"You're suddenly an expert on what's none of your damn business?"

My hands fisted under the table. If anything could trigger me to go off on him, it was Jace using the exact words he did on me when I was eight. Trying to control my temper, I didn't want him to know his words affected me.

Instead, I played it cool and stood.

Leaning close to his ear, I whispered, "You mean like you stealing and destroying my pack of cigarettes was yours?"

"You know one cigarette takes fourteen minutes off your life?"

"Like every time I'm around you? Well shit," I exclaimed, mocking him. "I must have lost years off my life just from you."

His brothers weren't paying us any mind. They were too busy flirting with women.

"Do you have a smart-ass response for everything I say?"

I narrowed my eyes at him and spoke with conviction, "I'd love to stand here and continue with this deadly conversation, but I don't want to waste any more of my time on you. Besides, I can't process how your delusional mind works, Jace, because I can't get my head that far up your ass."

And... he fucking smiled. A shit-eating grin I wanted to slap off his face.

"I wish I could say this was fun, but let's be honest, the pleasure was all yours. Now if you'll excuse me, I'm going to go flirt with men around my age because the last thing I want is for guys to think I'm hanging out with my father." I stepped aside to leave, but at the last second, he gripped my arm.

"Cove, use that snarky mouth on me again, and I'll give you something to bitch about."

I didn't hesitate in spewing...

"Don't start a war you can't win, G.I. Joe."

CHAPTER 3
COVE

I walked away, not giving him a second glance.

I made a beeline to the bar, using my fake ID to buy a beer. I waited for Haven to walk out of the bathroom, and once she did, I met her halfway and grabbed her hand to pull her onto the dance floor.

The crowd parted for us as the music switched from the live band to a DJ spinning the latest hits. People made it nearly impossible to dance. There was barely any space to move, which was always my favorite. I loved being the center of attention, and being a cheerleader for the last four years made it easy to know how to please a crowd.

It didn't take long for some pretty boy to come up behind me, and another guy I assumed was his friend gripped Haven's hips, working her ass on his dick as my beer splashed all over the floor by our feet.

"Relax, Haven!" I shouted over the music, feeling her anxiety about dancing with a man with her brothers near us. "Have some fun! We're just dancing."

I didn't care if they were a couple of feet away. It was one thing for Jace to snatch my cigarettes. He wouldn't play that same tune with me just from dancing with a guy. I wasn't his sister. There was no reason for him to treat me like I was.

Shoving the mere thought of him away from my mind, I started dancing on the guy, swaying my body to the beat of the music as his hands stayed on my hips. We moved in sync with one another. By the feel of the bulge in his pants, he liked it. A lot.

I got lost in the music and the feel of his hands on me until all of a sudden, I heard Haven exclaim, "Holy shit!"

At the last second, I saw her brothers shoving people out of the way as if a ticking time bomb was about to explode. I watched as they took down anyone in their path, needing to get to her as fast as they could.

"Oh my God," I rasped. "You have got to be kidding me."

Her brother Ledger's fist pulled back first, hitting the guy she was dancing with right in the jaw. Before I could scream at him for exaggerating what he just did, Jace unexpectedly hit the guy I was dancing with, causing my beer to splatter everywhere onto the ground.

In one quick movement, Reid threw Haven over his shoulder while Jace threw me over his.

"What the fuck?" I shrieked, caught off guard by what was happening. I immediately began waylaying on Jace's back, demanding he put me down. "Who the fuck do you think you are!"

The rest of her brothers stayed inside, going to war with those men for nothing. We were just dancing.

Why was I getting dragged into this? Jace never treated me this way before.

"Jace! Put me down!" I ordered. To say I was confused was an understatement. "Now!"

He did, slamming my feet to the ground so hard I had to put my hands on his chest for balance.

Not a second later, he roared, "Not another fucking word out of your mouth, Cove!"

Hearing his tone, I pushed him as hard as I could. "Fuck you!"

For the second time that day, he wrapped his hand around my throat, backing me into the building this time. He held me firmly in place with what could only be described as a death grip.

Before I could lay it on him for treating me like this, he declared, "You are such a bad example for Haven! You're nothing but bad news!"

"And you're such an overbearing asshole! She's eighteen, dickwad!"

"So are you! Why the hell are you drinking?"

"Because I can!" I tried to shove his hand away, but it didn't budge. "Jace, if you don't let go of me, I'll—"

"You'll what?" he sneered through a clenched jaw.

My chest heaved, feeling the weight of his insults and warning.

"You're going to be a good little girl and get your ass in my truck. Do you understand me?"

"Good little girl?" I emphasized, offended. "Are you for real?"

"When you act like a child, I'll treat you like one."

"A child? I'm an adult! I can do whatever I want. You're not my brother!"

"And thank God for that. I'd be ashamed if I were."

I winced. It was quick, but he saw it.

Haven must have too because she coaxed, "Jace—"

He silenced Haven with his finger in the air behind him. His seething glare didn't move from my furious expression.

"You want to parade your pussy around like it's fucking free? Then you'll meet men who won't hesitate to fuck you in the bathroom stall. Is that what you want for yourself, Cove?"

I flinched, taking in what he was brutally saying. No one had ever spoken to me this way.

"Jace, that's enough!" Haven ordered, knowing he was purposely hurting my feelings.

He didn't listen to her, not that I expected him to.

Fuck him.

"One day, you'll find yourself in a heap of trouble if you don't start changing your ways. Have more goddamn respect for yourself, little girl." With that, he let me go. "Now get your ass in my truck so I can drive you home."

I snapped, "I can take an Uber."

"Cove… I'm not going to tell you again."

My intense gaze shifted to Haven as she mouthed, "Just go with him."

Meeting his glare, I reminded, "I'm not your problem, Jace."

"I'm making you my problem."

Reluctantly, I left with him. However, that didn't stop him from grabbing my arm to guide me like a fucking lap dog.

"Jace, let go of me," I demanded, aware it would fall on deaf ears.

I tried keeping up with his stride as he rushed us to his big souped-up truck. The clicking sound of my heeled boots vibrated deep within my core with each step I took. One by one, it added to all the chaos erupting in my head.

"You're going too fast," I pleaded. "You're going to make me break my ankle."

"Then maybe next time you'll think twice about wearing fuck-me boots to a bar where men only want to fuck you in them."

"News flash, asshole! We came here with you."

He stopped dead in his tracks, turning to face me. "Yes, *with me.* What part of that did you not understand?"

"Why does it matter if I drink and dance with a guy? I do it all the time."

"You should have known better than to do it in front of me."

"Okay, enough with the G.I. Joe bullshit, Jace. I don't need you to be my soldier."

"I can protect your country, but not your pussy?"

My mouth dropped open.

"If you're going to portray yourself like a piece of ass, then men will treat you like one."

I sassed, "I guess that's not present company excluded?"

"Don't compare me to a man who'd ever fuck you, Cove."

"You're right," I snarled. "I'm too good for you."

"Don't get it twisted. Your insults don't faze me. If anything, all it proves is how lost you really are."

"I'm not lost. I know exactly who I am. I don't need you to save me, Jace. I've been doing it my entire life. I can take care of myself. Now if you'll take your hand off me, I won't have to knee you in the balls."

If he had any reaction to what I just shared, he didn't show it.

Cold.

Detached.

Soulless.

That was all he showed me.

"Get your ass in my truck, or I'll throw your ass in. Either way, I'm driving you home."

I didn't have a choice in the matter, and I hated that more than anything. The ride to my house was quiet, but on the way there, I needed to use the bathroom.

"Can you pull over at the next gas station?"

"I didn't hear the word please."

My jaw clenched. "Please."

Shortly after, he pulled up to a gas pump and turned off the engine.

"You have ten minutes, or I'm coming in after you."

"You go from G.I. Joe to military sergeant? How about you give me the itinerary of what personality will come out of you next?"

He opened his door. "You're down to nine minutes. I'd hurry if I were you."

I rolled my eyes, jumping out of his truck.

On my way to the bathroom, I ran into someone, and my bag was knocked to the floor, spilling everything inside it.

"Shit!" I crouched down, quickly throwing my things back in before dickwad appeared and further embarrassed me in front of strangers.

"Dammit." The man I collided with bent down with me.

"I'm sorry. That was my fault. Here, let me help you."

"You don't have to—" Glancing up, I was rendered speechless as soon as I locked eyes with the gorgeous guy in front of me.

He smiled, and I swear my heart fluttered. His pearly white teeth and bright-green eyes were mesmerizing. Not to mention, he had dimples, and his black leather jacket only heightened the scent of his intoxicating cologne.

I swallowed hard, immediately captivated by his whole demeanor.

"What was that?" he asked, eyeing me up and down.

"Hi," I nervously announced. "I'm Cove."

"Nice to meet you, Cove. I'm Deacon."

Jesus… even his name was hot.

"What's a pretty girl like you doing hanging out in a gas station by herself?"

"Umm…" Suddenly feeling panicked that Jace would interrupt this moment and ruin it for me, I stressed, "I'd love to continue this conversation, but my ride is with an asshole, and I have to go."

"Do you need me to put him in his place for you?"

My stomach somersaulted with how he was instantly in protective mode over me.

"He's my best friend's much older brother. I mean, he's so old he could be my father, so no need to defend me, but I appreciate it."

"How about you give me your number so I can take you out to dinner instead?"

Haven hated when I was reckless and gave guys I didn't know my number, but I was a live-in-the-moment kind of girl, and I wasn't going to miss the opportunity for my very own bad boy.

"I'd love that."

I gave him what he wanted, knowing with certainty he'd call. I just never expected he'd text me when I was still in Jace's truck.

I'm going to think about you for the rest of my night.

And the truth was…

I was thinking about him too.

CHAPTER 4
COVE
NOW: ONE MONTH LATER

I laughed, "Deacon," as he blew raspberries on my belly while holding me down on his couch. "Stop torturing me!"

"It's not torture when you like it, beauty."

I smiled despite wanting to toss him off me. He started calling me beauty from the second he picked me up on our first date.

Holding my wrists above my head, he baited, "What do I get if I stop?"

"What do you want?"

"Now those are my favorite words."

"You're horrible. You know that, right?"

He released me. "It's why you like me."

"It's why I shouldn't."

"Beauty, we both know you would be devastated if you didn't have

30

me in your life."

Before the last word left his mouth, I knocked him in the face with a pillow.

His eyes went wide. "Oh, beauty, it's on now."

I shrieked, about to block his attack, but I was too slow. He went straight for my inner thigh.

"Deacon, don't you dare," I warned as his finger dug into my skin.

"You can't do this! You can't—"

"Try to stop me, beauty."

I pitifully tried to shove his hand away. "You always do this. You always tickle me. It isn't fair!"

"What's not fair? That you love it? Is that what's not fair?"

"No!"

He grinned, squeezing my thigh again, and I lost my shit. Kicking my legs, I flailed everywhere, and my body shook uncontrollably from his assault.

I would not laugh. I could not laugh.

It'd only entice him.

He squeezed harder, twitching his fingers on the muscle to the point of pain. Like when you hit your damn funny bone—it hurt like a bitch, but it made you laugh from the sting. I couldn't take it anymore, and I squealed, laughing hysterically and screaming all at the same time. His body firmly locked on top of mine, giving him the advantage to continue to torture me unmercifully and with no remorse.

"Deacon! You're going to make me pee my pants!"

He pressed harder, my throat burned, and my voice sounded hoarse.

"You have five seconds to apologize for hitting me in the face."

"With a pillow!"

"Four seconds, or I'll really have no mercy on you at all. Three... two..."

I fought harder and laughed louder.

"One…"

"I'm sorry!" I screamed, trying to catch my breath, and he finally stopped.

I exhaled heavily, in and out, my chest rising and falling, with my heart pounding out of my skin. My warm body had sweat forming at my temples.

With the back of his fingers, he swept the hair away from my eyes.

"You're still horrible."

"And you still like me."

"I don't know why."

"Sure, you do. Who else can make you feel like this?"

He kissed me slowly and passionately. I'd never been kissed like he'd kiss me. Every time his lips touched mine, a deep spark would ignite in the core of my body and in the center of my heart. For the first time in my life, I was falling in love, and the feeling was very much mutual.

I felt it in my bones.

This man was falling for me too.

Finally, I found what I'd been looking for.

I giggled, feeling the weight of him on me. It was one of my favorite things in the world.

"You're squishing me."

"But I'm so comfortable."

"You're such a bully in so many languages."

"Feisty words for someone who just lost our battle."

"I always lose the battle."

"Yet you still try me every chance you get."

"I can't help you're a bully in your heart and soul, Deacon McKay."

"Well, Cove Trinity Noel, I guess that makes you my prey."

"I like the sound of that."

"Do you have any idea how fucking beautiful you are?"

"I do." I smiled. "But tell me anyway."

He kissed me again. "You feel so fucking good beneath me, beauty."

We'd been spending a lot of time together. With Hayes taking up most of Haven's time, I filled mine with Deacon. He spoiled me with his complete attention. I wasn't used to being with a guy who wanted to know every last thing about me. He wasn't just asking to ask. He was genuinely invested in everything I willingly shared with him.

It was nice to feel like the center of someone's universe.

I never had that before.

In the last month alone—he was attentive, caring, and constantly surprising me with trips to places he knew I loved because I told him. He took me to the zoo for a private tour with the animals, a behind-the-scenes experience, and it was amazing.

We spent a weekend in the Grand Canyon, where he rented us a high-end tent, and we watched the stars at night while hiking during the day. I loved nature. Anytime I could be outside, I was. He even woke up at four o'clock on our last day there so we could watch the sunrise over the horizon.

Every last detail of my favorite things to do he accomplished. He was effortlessly checking off all my boxes. I couldn't help but fall in love with him. Especially since we hadn't had sex yet. He said he wanted to wait until I was ready. Making out was as far as we went, and he was content enough with it. It truly blew my mind how patient he was with me.

He was twenty-eight and an engineer for the biggest oil company in town. Based on his cabin home in the mountains, he made a great living. His parents were retired, spending most of their time traveling. He didn't see them often and was an only child like me. We bonded over that. He knew firsthand what it felt like to be lonely, having a similar upbringing as mine.

Changing the subject, he questioned, "You want to tell me what this morning was about and why you had to leave my bed so damn early?"

I crashed at his place more often than not. It beat having to be alone in the massive estate that was my childhood home.

"Oh... umm... don't worry about it."

"That sounds reassuring."

"Yeah... it's fine. It's just Haven dealing with Hayes again."

A week after we started hanging out, Jace blew up my phone to find his sister one night. Haven spent the evening making up with Hayes and put her phone on Airplane Mode so they wouldn't be interrupted.

Hence, Jace showed up at my house and left the nastiest note on my car, thinking I was hiding something from him regarding Haven. Deacon didn't appreciate the sentiment, and ever since then, he was extremely protective over me in reference to her brother.

His possessiveness really showed how much he cared, or at least it did to me. It was such a turn-on, and I loved it.

"What happened?"

I shrugged. "Long story."

"I have time."

I threw my arms around his neck. "Then we shouldn't be wasting it on their drama, but..." I smirked. "I did tell her about you."

"Oh yeah?" He grinned, his dimples proudly on display. "What did you tell her?"

"That I met my very own bad boy."

"Is that right?" He kissed me before adding, "Is everything okay, or is her brother still giving you shit?"

I rolled my eyes. "I can handle Jace."

"So can I."

I giggled. "I don't need you to protect me from Jace."

"And why is that?"

I tried to shift the conversation. "Have I told you how much I love that you're an alpha?"

"Beauty, you have no idea."

"I'm such a lucky girl."

"I'm the one who's lucky."

I beamed, kissing him again.

"Don't think I don't know what you're doing. Now are you going to tell me the truth about Jace?"

"There's nothing to tell. Honestly, I don't really know him that well."

"But he knows you enough to speak to you the way he does?"

"He talks to everyone like that."

"Trust me, beauty. If he keeps fucking around, he'll find out your boyfriend—"

"Boyfriend?" I blurted, surprised he used that word.

He cocked his head to the side, narrowing his gaze intently on me.

"What?" I breathed out, unable to hold back with needing to know the reason for the sudden tension in the room.

Staring deep into my eyes, he professed in a sharp tone, "Cove, you're mine."

My lips parted. "I like the sound of that."

Within seconds, a whole new set of unexpected emotions burst inside me when he revealed for the first time, "I love you, beauty."

I didn't hesitate to confess…

"I love you too."

CHAPTER 5
JACE
THEN: ONE YEAR AFTER THE FUNERAL

After eleven years in the Navy, I was on my fifth deployment overseas. I hadn't been home since we buried our mother. Nothing else mattered but my duty to my country. It was the only thing I had left inside me after her death.

Which, ironically, had me claiming more lives of the enemy, causing me to lose myself a little more each day.

"Seriously, man," Tony, one of my commanders in my unit, coaxed, pulling me away from my thoughts.

"I can't wait to get back home. I'm going to ask my girl to marry me. Did I tell you she was pregnant?"

I barely listened to him. I was on high alert, glancing around the empty streets with him following me as the rest of my unit was in the opposite alley, surrounding the building we were patrolling. For the past few years, Tony had been my closest friend. He watched my six, and I watched his.

For the past three months, it was the same old bullshit every single day on repeat. I embarked on endless foot-patrol missions that would last for two to three weeks at a time. It always felt like we were being watched in one way or another. We had our finger on the trigger at all times, ready to unleash at any given moment.

The days were long, and the nights even longer.

The crazy part about it was that being back in these missions almost felt like home to me. We all felt this way. At the end of the day, being a civilian was much harder than being a soldier. Our minds were always on the battlefield, along with the souls we'd taken.

In the times I was home, it was hard to readjust to normal life, and that was the hardest pill to swallow. It was so difficult to switch your normalcy back on. I lived and breathed a life where I was under constant attack.

I killed enemies.

I lost soldiers.

The long periods of violence took a psychological toll on me mentally. I'd wake up several times throughout the night, freaking the fuck out if I couldn't find my gun, even if I didn't need it at that moment.

I was always waiting for the other shoe to drop, always on alert, always waiting to kill what I couldn't fucking see, hear, or touch. These missions all required the same thing, which only a handful of Elite Force teams could pull off.

The team I was in charge of was the best of the fucking best—a group of ruthless men who feared nothing. Our rifles were loaded and fucking ready to shoot, stepping one foot in front of each other, listening all around for any sign of the fuckers.

I put my left hand up, signaling to continue. "All clear," I informed through my radio.

As I looked through my scope, turning right and left, we trucked through the woods, trying to be as invisible as possible. Blending in with nature. Not even my breathing could get out of sync. The more treacherous the situation, the calmer I was.

See, my worst nightmare had already come true. Nothing was left for me to fear but fear itself.

My adrenaline worked overtime, knowing the enemy was close, but I had no visual at all. All my actions and orders needed to be calculated and precise. My hearing only heightened with every step I took toward the direction of danger.

Suddenly, an eerie feeling I recognized all too well crept up my spine. I looked around us, moving out in front of Tony. For a second, I thought I saw movement out of the corner of my eye, but then a gust of wind blinded me with the dirt in the stale, dry air.

"Did you hear that?" I whispered loud enough for him to hear.

He nodded behind me. "Did you see that shit?"

I did see it.

I saw everything but didn't need to turn my head to know what he was referring to. It happened so fast, yet it seemed so fucking slow.

I drew my gun at the exact moment I caught a sniper out of the corner of my eye, aiming his shot right toward Tony. Springing into action as if on autopilot, I shoved him back as hard as I could with my gun out in front of me. The sharp, familiar sound of a bullet whistling through the desert air just missed the back of my head and flew into the concrete building.

I regained my balance, taking out the sniper before he had a chance to kill either of us. I shot a bullet in the center of his forehead like it was just another day.

Abruptly, screams echoed in the distance, halting my descent.

"Fuck!" I shouted through my radio. "Get down!" The sons of bitches opened rapid fire on us.

There was no time to think.

No time to breathe.

No time to get the fuck out of there.

"Fuck you!" Tony seethed. "NO!" I screamed bloody murder, fully aware of what was about to go down.

He returned the favor, shoving me out of the way.

"Tony, don't—"

BAM!

His body instantly jolted back from the impact of the bullet in the side of his neck.

My strength.

My will to keep fucking going.

"Shit," I sputtered. Carefully, I turned over to my stomach, fighting a war with my body to do what it was trained to. I slowly sat up, crawling toward a nearby tree until I leaned against it.

After my eyes adjusted back into focus from sunlight and the dirty air, I blinked a few times, gradually looking up. Adjusting to the light, I looked all around me, needing to find Tony. I desperately pushed through the disorientation and confusion of our location and where Tony's body could have been tossed.

Several explosions continued to go off nearby, and it felt as if the seconds turned into minutes and minutes turned into hours. I was frantically trying to see where he was. I pushed off the tree, stumbling to stand on my own. I placed one foot in front of the other, repeating in my head, *I need to find him.*

My body was obviously going into shock as I tried to make my way toward Tony. A man who'd become like a brother to me. It was only then I saw that he wasn't moving. The closer I got to him, I maneuvered on autopilot as I hurried down the alleyway. I didn't give a fuck about anything else but getting to him.

Guns blazing.

Bullets firing in all directions.

Hell had broken loose around me, yet it didn't bother me anymore.

I didn't think anything could faze me until I came upon his body. So much blood came out of what was left of him as he convulsed, shaking uncontrollably. I watched him dying right in front of my tormented stare. I didn't think twice about it. I grabbed him, dragging his limp form to what appeared to be a vacant shed. Ignoring his pleas of desperation not to move him, he urgently begged me to just leave him there. I stopped once we were far enough inside the shitty walls and away from any points of entry. I hid us as best as I could for the time being until one of my men could find us. Everything blended together, including my goddamn sanity.

"Jace, I can't..." he bellowed in a tone that wasn't his, already giving up on life.

"It's fine, Tony. I've got you, buddy. You're going to be just fine." I hovered above him, shielding his frame with mine. I desperately tried to keep my emotions in check.

"Jace..."

I swallowed hard, shutting my eyes for a few seconds, needing a minute to get my shit together to look down at him again.

I mentally prepared myself for what I would experience, for what would happen, for what I knew he was going to beg me for because I would plead for the same fucking thing if I were in his position. I peered down at the soldier I'd known for what felt like a lifetime, taking in my best fucking friend. "I'm here, brother. I'm here," I gritted out, my lips trembling.

"Do it..." He bled out through his mouth. "I can't die like this... please... just do it for me..."

I reached over and grabbed his hand, squeezing it. I provided any comfort I could, letting him know I was there with him.

"Tell my girl sweet pea I love her, okay?"

I nodded, hanging on by a thread.

"Tell my kid one day that I died a hero, okay?"

"Of course. I swear to you they'll be taken care of."

He started to cough up clots of blood. I tried to sit him up, but he screamed in misery.

I nodded, unable to form words. "I'm sorry, Tony. I'm so fucking sorry. It's my job to protect my team, and I failed you." I bowed my head in shame.

His body began convulsing, this time worse than the last.

"Jace... let me die with honor..."

Another gasp of air gurgled in his lungs. He was suffocating in his own blood.

With my fingers, I shut his eyes and did what I had to do.

I pulled out my Glock, shut my eyes, and ended his misery. And just like that, in the blink of an eye.

Tony saved my life while I claimed his.

CHAPTER 6
COVE
NOW: ALMOST TWO MONTHS LATER

"**Y**ou're going to make me go to Grad Weekend without you?" I asked, throwing my hiking boots in my luggage.

We were three weeks away from graduation, and Grad Weekend was finally here. Our class, along with several others in the state, were going to Disney Springs in Yellowstone for the next two days.

"I would never be able to forgive myself if I made you miss this weekend to stay with me. You've been looking forward to it since ninth grade."

I sighed. "You would get the flu now."

"Right? Like what the hell?"

"Are you sure you don't want me to stay with you?"

"Stop asking me that. I already told you no. All I want is for you to have so much fun and take lots of pictures and videos. I'll be stalking your social media with a severe case of FOMO."

"I promise I will. Don't forget to keep me updated on how you're feeling."

"I'm fine. The doctor said I have a mild case, and I'll be good as new in a couple of days."

"Fine. Just promise me you'll wash your damn hair and change out of those stinky sweats you've been wearing since you and Hayes broke up."

"Stop hating on my sweats, Cove. They're in style now."

"Yeah, to go to the airport in, not to live in."

"All I want to do is lie in bed and watch movies all weekend."

I threw my toiletry bag in my luggage next. "If you watch *The Notebook* one more fucking time, Haven, so help me God…"

"It's a classic, Cove."

"Watch *Titanic*, that bitch could have shared the door with Jack, and we all know it. Now that's the mood you need to be in." I zipped up my suitcase. "Oh! What about your dad? Is he not chaperoning anymore?"

"He's going to—"

"Hey, Deacon's beeping in. Since I'll be alone in my hotel room now, I'm going to try to convince him to come stay with me tonight."

"Wait a second. Isn't that against school policy?"

"Rules were made to be broken, Haven."

"Cove, don't get in trouble three weeks before graduation."

"I've already accepted my admission to Wyoming University. I can't get in trouble. Besides, everyone will be trying to sneak into each other's rooms. It's part of the fun of it all."

"Cove—"

"Relax. You know I've been sneaking people into my bedroom since middle school. I'm a pro at this point."

"That's why there are chaperones. I'm sure there will be one on every floor."

"They have to pee at some point, don't they?"

"Cove—"

"Living on the edge makes life worth living, Haven. Love you! Byeeee…" I hung up, answering Deacon, "Hey, babe."

"Hey, beauty. Are you packed and ready to go?"

"I am."

"Have I told you how much I'm going to miss you?"

"You won't have to miss me. Haven's sick, so it looks like I'll have our room all to myself."

"Is that right?"

"Mm-hmm. Maybe you'll even get lucky."

"Beauty, you're not ready."

I rolled my eyes. "Isn't that my decision to make?"

"What kind of man would I be if I fucked you before you were ready?"

The man had the patience of a saint. We made out a lot, but he'd stop any time we got close to the next step.

"The kind who gives his girlfriend countless orgasms."

"My cock doesn't have to be inside you to do that."

"Prove it."

"We'll see."

"Does that mean you're coming?"

"Maybe."

"I'll take it."

Once we hung up, I drove to school just in the nick of time for the school buses to be leaving. After leaving my luggage with the driver, I went inside. I stopped dead in my tracks when I saw the person I least expected sitting in the seat right next to mine.

"Oh. Fuck. No." I stressed, shaking my head.

Jace smiled wide, folding his arms over his chest. "Cove, for this weekend, it's Mr. Beckham to you."

I glared at him. "You're filling in for your father, aren't you?"

He patted the seat next to him. "Saved it for you."

"Old people sit in the front of the bus, G.I. Joe."

He arched an eyebrow, ordering in a stern voice, "Sit."

"I'm not your dog, let alone your bitch."

"That's where you're wrong." He tossed a lanyard at me that read, *Mr. Beckham's Assistant.*

"Shit."

"Now sit."

"I didn't sign up to be *your* assistant. Haven and I were your dad's."

"Well, I've replaced him, so now that makes you mine."

"Absolutely not. I'm going to request a—"

"Cove! There you are," Mrs. Myer exclaimed, walking over to me.

"I see you've found out that you'll be assisting Mr. Beckham's son instead this weekend."

"Yeah, about that—"

"Since Haven had requested a joined room with her father—"

"Right, I forgot about that."

"The only rooms the hotel can accommodate on such short notice are two adjoining rooms with a privacy door."

"Oh… so I'll have my own room?"

"Yes."

Thinking back on Deacon, I figured it'd be much easier for me to sneak him in if I had my own room.

"That sounds great. Thank you."

By the abrupt change in my tune, Jace eyed me skeptically.

"Perfect." She smiled.

After she stepped away, I reluctantly sat down next to Jace.

"Remind me to yell at Haven for not giving me the heads-up that you'd be here."

"She didn't know."

"Whatever."

Disney Springs was only an hour away, thank God. I threw in my AirPods and paid him no mind until we pulled into the Springs. I was the first to break the silence between us, unable to hold back any longer.

"Why are you even here?" I refused to look at him, keeping my attention focused in front of me. "Don't you have friends your own age? Why would you want to hang out with a bunch of high school kids?"

"I thought you were an adult?"

"You know what I mean." I gestured to the bus. "This doesn't exactly seem like your speed. Isn't there a senior citizen event you're missing out on this weekend?"

He ignored my dig. "I'm doing my father a favor. If you weren't such a spoiled brat, you'd know what that was."

I turned to face him. "What's your problem?"

"Nothing. I'm just stating the obvious."

"You know nothing about me."

"I know everything I need to know."

"Which is what?"

"You don't want to go down this road with me, Cove."

"Try me."

When he didn't say a word, I continued. "Fine. I'll go first. Why do you always act like you have a permanent stick up your ass? Better yet, why are you always treating Haven like she's a baby who can't fend for herself? Have you seen her lately? She's devastated about Hayes."

"How many times do I have to tell you to mind your own damn business?"

"As many as it takes to get you off her back."

46

"And you think this is the way to do it?"

"As a matter of fact, I do. You keep telling me to mind my own damn business. Well, you need to as well to make it fair."

"Hate to break it to you, bunny. Life's not fair."

I jerked back. "Bunn—"

The school bus came to a quick stop, cutting me off. Before I could ask where that nickname came from, he stood, nodding for us to go. I did as I was told, mostly from being caught off guard by what he had just called me.

I shook off the sentiment, reaching for my luggage, but Jace grabbed it for me. I couldn't help but notice how strong he was. He picked up my bag and his as if they weighed nothing.

By the time I walked into my hotel room, it was almost lunchtime, and we were supposed to meet in Mickey's private suite for our class only in an hour. I took a quick rinse, and as I was wrapping the towel around my body, there was a knock on my door.

"I'm coming!" Making sure the towel was secure, I opened the door to find Jace standing on the other side.

"This is how you answer the door?" he immediately reprimanded.

"Of course not. If I knew you were standing behind it, I wouldn't have opened it at all."

I don't know what bothered me more—the fact that he was mad I opened the door in a towel or the fact that he didn't even look at me while I was standing wet and practically naked in front of him. His eyes did not glance down at my body for one second—it was like I was nothing more than a child to him.

"What do you want?"

"For you to put some fucking clothes on."

"No problem." I slammed the door in his face. "Asshole."

I returned to my bathroom to get dressed and put on some makeup. I never imagined when I stepped back into my room…

Jace would be leaning against the doorframe of our adjoining rooms.

CHAPTER 7
COVE
NOW: ONE MONTH LATER

"**T**his is breaking and entering, Jace."

"What part of adjoining rooms do you not understand?"

"The part where you're standing in *my* room uninvited."

"I don't need an invitation when you're my assistant for the weekend."

"This is bullshit. Why would you want to be around me all weekend? You don't even like me."

"Don't put words in my mouth I've never said."

"You could've fooled me, but you know what? That doesn't change the fact that *I* hate you. So why don't you go find another cheerleader to be at your beck and call for the next two days?"

"No," he stated. "I want you."

"You say that like you mean it."

"I never say anything I don't mean. You're my assistant." He pushed off the doorframe, walking toward me in a calculating stride. "I'm here to claim you, bunny."

Claim me? Why did that sound sexual?

Each step that brought him closer to me made my heart accelerate.

"I...I..."

"You what?"

"Why do you keep calling me bunny?"

"Because it's better than me calling you a pain in my ass."

"You're in my room, and I'm the pain in the ass?"

He grinned, standing in front of me. "Are you always this quick-witted?"

"It's part of my charm."

"Here, I thought I brought out the worst in you."

"Oh!" I mocked in a condescending tone. "Here, I thought you knew everything about me?"

"Why do you insist on fighting with me?"

"Why do you insist on pissing me off so much? Last time we spoke, I was a slut who was a bad example for your sister, remember?"

"A slut would actually spread her legs and not just pretend to."

"What's that supposed to mean?"

"You're a cock tease, Cove, and not because you're genuinely interested in lying on your back for a random boy. You're simply trying to find validation in all the wrong places. It's why you're still a virgin."

My mouth dropped open. "You have no right—"

"Truth hurts, bunny. I warned you on the bus to stop baiting me, but I'll lay it out for you since you don't know how to take no for an answer. I'm not afraid to hurt your feelings, which only has about a five-second delay before you're back to being a pain in my ass."

"You assho—"

"Let me finish," he ordered, further infuriating me.

"You need to stop pretending to be someone you're not. It will end badly for you if you continue down this path just because you're lonely and looking for attention from the wrong people."

Feeling naive, I lied, "I'm not a virgin."

He eyed me up and down for a moment. "People blink less when they're lying and blink more after they lie, so try that again with less deception this time."

"So now you're Sherlock Holmes?"

"If I told you"—he grinned again—"I'd have to kill you."

I swallowed hard.

"You nervous, bunny?"

"No." I quickly blinked twice. "Shit."

He scoffed out a chuckle.

"So what? You're like a walking lie detector?"

"Something like that."

My eyebrows pinched together.

"Stop weighing your words."

"Then get out of my head."

"But you make it so damn easy, Cove."

"You don't know anything about me. Stop generalizing me with your statistics of case studies. They have nothing to do with me."

He purposely stepped toward me, expecting me to step back.

I didn't.

"What part don't I know? You're impulsive, and you think you're grown."

"So does every eighteen-year-old who's ever lived."

"Alright… how about this?"

This man was full of surprises. "You move your hair to cover the side

51

of your face when you're anxious. You fidget with your fingers when you're deep in thought. You bite your fingernails when you think no one is looking. You smile when you're hurting. You hate to admit when you're wrong. You laugh when you're uncomfortable and pretend you don't need anyone. In reality, you're just looking for a boy to fill that void that Daddy never gave you."

I narrowed my eyes at him as my heart accelerated, pounding profusely in my chest.

"Here's a good one. You have tons of thoughts running through your mind right now, but the main one is how much you want to push me away. I'm the first man to call you out on your bullshit, and that scares you more than anything. I see right through you, Cove. And like a bunny, you're just hoping someone will go down that rabbit hole with you because at least then, you won't be alone anymore."

With my heart in my throat, I asked, "How do you know all that?"

He didn't hesitate to speak with conviction. "I'm trained to."

"You're not in the military anymore. You don't need to—"

"That's where you're wrong. My mind is always at war with itself. It's the consequence of taking souls that didn't belong to me."

I didn't know what to say.

What to feel.

I could barely contemplate what he willingly just shared with me.

This was the most I'd ever learned about him. His family never spoke about what he did for the past twenty years. There was so much more I wanted to know and ask, but I knew he wouldn't answer my questions, even if I begged him to.

For the first time since I met him, I felt like his walls were momentarily down, which messed with my head more than I wanted to admit.

I was no longer that little girl whose heart he'd broken.

At that moment, I was the woman who understood him.

The silence was deafening, hammering repeatedly in my core and throughout my entire body. The weight of his words hung heavy in the room as I tried to find more answers through his eyes.

Except Jace was a soldier. He wouldn't show me anything unless he wanted to. I couldn't see past his shield of armor that was once again proudly displayed before me.

"Is this what I have to do to shut you up?"

I couldn't stop from blurting, "I'm sorry that happened to you, Jace."

Stepping back, he bit, "I don't need your pity, Cove."

"What about my sympathy?"

"I need that even less."

"You know this tough guy act isn't healthy."

"It's not an act."

I shrugged. "I'm just trying to help you."

"The only help I need from you is your assisting skills this weekend."

"Fine. Have it your way."

He spent the next twenty minutes filling me in on what he needed. Except I was barely listening. I was too hyper focused on what he just shared with me.

"It's the consequence of taking souls that didn't belong to me."

Only then did I realize there was so much more to Jace Beckham than met the eye. I couldn't help but want to know what else lay beneath his hard exterior.

After lunch, our weekend coordinator took my class around the ranch while riding horses. I'd be lying if I said I wasn't watching Jace's skills and how effortlessly he rode his horse, remembering all the times I saw him on one when he was helping his father around their ranch.

To make matters worse, all the girls drooled over him, waiting for him to pay attention to them. It was truly pitiful to watch, and for some reason, it annoyed me to see how much the girls fawned over him.

Once the tour was over, I used the bathroom in the stables.

As I washed my hands, a fellow cheerleader on my squad came into view of my mirror.

"There you are," Gaby greeted. "I need you to tell me everything about Jace!"

"Uh… why would I know anything about him?"

"Oh, come on! He's Haven's brother, and you're practically sisters. Now spill."

"Honest, Gaby. I don't know much about him."

"Do you at least know if he has a girlfriend?"

Does he?

"I'm not sure."

"We have the campfire tonight. Can you save me a seat next to him?"

My eyebrows pinched together. "Aren't you with Jordan?"

"Why would I want to be with a boy when I can be with a man?"

"Does Jordan know about that?"

"Who cares. He's not here this weekend."

I snidely spewed, "That's nice."

"Why are you being so weird about helping me with Jace? Do you like him or something?"

"No."

"No?"

"Of course not. He's my best friend's brother."

"So if he wasn't you'd be into him?"

Would I?

I shot down the thought. "Absolutely not."

"Great! Don't forget to save me a seat." With that, she turned and left.

The entire time we were at the campfire, I watched her practically throw herself at him. Although Jace seemed indifferent toward her, it didn't stop the unexpected jealousy I felt seeing her try to entice him.

I'd never seen Jace with a woman before, and it was a hard pill to swallow. I hadn't thought about him in a romantic way since I was a kid, and it was fucking with the hatred I thought I still had for him.

He asked, "What's wrong?"

I played it off. "I'm fine."

"You don't look fine."

"I thought you knew everything about me?"

He narrowed his eyes at me before looking at Gaby, who hung her marshmallow over the fire a few feet away from us.

She glanced back at him smiling, making me roll my eyes.

"You don't like her?" he questioned, only loud enough for me to hear.

Shit! Could he sense my jealousy?

"She's fine."

"And you're obviously not."

"Stop psychoanalyzing me."

When his stare became too much, I abruptly stood. "I'm going to bed."

"It's only eight."

"So?"

Jesus, Cove… that's your best comeback?

"You're a night owl."

"What the fuck?" I shook my head. "Are you secretly stalking me?"

"My bedroom was next to Haven's, remember? You two love to stay up all night."

"Is there anything you don't know? You want to tell me when my next cycle is?"

"Based on your bitchy attitude, I'd say you're PMSing right now, so it should be soon."

My eyes widened.

"Don't ask questions you don't want answers to, bunny."

"On that note, I'm going to bed."

"Cove—"

I should have kept my mouth shut, but once again, I couldn't help myself. "FYI, Gaby has a boyfriend."

He cocked his head to the side, arching an eyebrow, and I immediately regretted my words.

"Why is that my concern?"

I shrugged. "I'd hate for you to hook up—"

"She's a kid. I'm a man. I don't fuck high schoolers."

"We graduate in—"

"We?"

Shit!

"You know what? You're right. You could be *our* father."

The expression on his face only proved he saw right through my bullshit. Feeling like I was literally under a microscope, I bowed my head.

"I'll see you tomorrow."

I didn't give him a chance to reply, getting the hell out of there instead. The elevator ride up to my room was slow and torturous for my state of mind.

What was wrong with me? Why was I jealous of Jace and Gaby? Why did I care?

It made no sense. Nothing did.

I hurried into my room, quickly shutting the door behind me to lean my forehead against it. Taking a deep breath, I felt overwhelmed by the turn in events.

I love Deacon, don't I?

For what felt like the hundredth time that day, I was caught off guard when two strong arms wrapped around my waist. Not thinking twice about it, I threw my head back into their face.

"What the fuck, Cove?"

I immediately recognized that voice.

CHAPTER 8
COVE

I snapped around. "Oh my God! Deacon, I'm so sorry."

He held his nose as blood seeped through his fingers, causing me to feel much worse.

"Shit! Let me get you some ice."

I ran to the bathroom for a washcloth before grabbing ice from the fridge.

He sat on the edge of the bed, angling his head back as I gently placed the ice on top of his nose for him.

"I'm so sorry. I didn't know it was you."

"I'd hope so."

"I thought you were trying to hurt me. How did you get in my room?"

"Who taught you how to do that?"

"Haven's brother Reid. He taught us a couple of self-defense moves when we grew boobs."

He chuckled.

Thank God, his nose stopped bleeding.

"I don't know whether to be mad or proud of you."

"Are you okay?"

"Yeah, it's just my dignity that took a hit."

"How did you get in my room?"

"I wanted to surprise you."

"I get that, but how did you—"

Moving the ice away from his nose, he stood. "Don't worry about it. Nobody saw me come in."

"That doesn't answer my question."

"How about you kiss me instead?"

I smiled, standing on my tippy-toes to peck him, but for the first time in my life, I envisioned Jace's lips on mine.

What the hell?

"I'll be right back. I'm going to wash up."

While he was in the bathroom, I frantically paced around the room.

"She's a kid. I'm a man. I don't fuck high schoolers."

I'd show him, throwing on a pink set of my bra and panties I grabbed my cell phone and pressed play on my sexy playlist I practiced my stripper moves to. I'd been taking a class for the past year, loving any dancing I could learn.

As soon as Deacon walked back in, I threw my arms around his neck. "Let me make it up to you."

Our kiss quickly turned heated until he abruptly pulled away. "Beauty…" he warned as I tried to move him closer to me by his shirt.

"Oh, come on, you want to waste this room?"

It was nightfall. The bright full moon loomed over the horizon like a beacon. Slowly, I spun around until my back was to his front. Swaying my hips side to side, I slid my hands up to my head to run my fingers seductively through my hair as I lifted it off my neck.

There was a strong shift in the air, the space, the energy all around us. Every inch of my skin stirred with an awakening.

My breathing hitched.

My pulse accelerated.

My heart started pounding out of my chest.

I licked my lips, my mouth suddenly dry. I got lost in the overpowering emotions about Jace that felt as if they were taking over me even though I was in Deacon's arms.

Shaking off the sentiment, I vowed, "I love you."

I did, didn't I?

He spun me to face him. "I love you too."

"Just be with me, okay? I know you want to."

"It's too risky. What if someone hears us?"

"I'll be quiet."

"That doesn't exactly do it for me."

"Come on… it's the thrill of it all."

"I thought you said you had your own room." He nodded toward the adjoining door.

"Don't worry about that."

"What if they—"

"I'll let you put it anywhere."

I could feel him grinning against my cheek.

"How about you let me persuade you?"

"Cove, I should go. I thought you had your own room."

I pushed him onto the bed, making him chuckle.

"I do. Now stop and enjoy this."

"Why are you being so persistent? What's going on with my girl?"

Since I couldn't confess the truth, I lied, "I just don't want to wait anymore."

Before he could tell me no, I unbuckled his belt and jeans.

"What are you doing?"

"Exactly what it looks like. If you won't touch me, then I'm going to touch you." I kissed along his stomach, trying to pull down his jeans.

"Beauty—"

"Shhh! I'm busy."

I tugged at his boxers, but he hastily flipped me over onto my back. Almost instantly, I was engulfed in his familiar, husky, masculine scent. Deacon's lips glided along the crook of my neck, and I gradually tilted my head, leaning away to allow him more access.

Meeting his eyes, I moved my hips against his dick, and he wrapped his strong arm around my waist, tugging me closer to him. Close enough to where there was nothing between us, only the friction of our heady movements.

It seemed like hours passed by, and all I wanted was to forget about Jace fucking Beckham.

Deacon gripped my ass, and I wrapped my legs around his waist, moaning into his mouth. He kissed me passionately, but my mind was still somewhere else entirely.

"Is this what you want, beauty?"

"Yes…"

He kissed his way down my neck, never taking his eyes off mine. Grinning like a fool, he pecked his lips down my chest, stomach, and inner thighs. My back arched off the bed while my hand went to the back of his neck.

"Fuck," he rasped, beginning to lower the seam of my panties.

This was the furthest we'd ever gone, and I was suddenly nervous about what would happen. I sat up to tell him that maybe I wasn't ready when the adjoining doorknob jiggled.

My eyes widened.

My heart dropped.

I swear I stopped breathing.

Jace shouted, "Cove, why is the door locked?"

"Who's that?" Deacon asked, abruptly standing as he buckled his pants.

Instantly, I jumped off the bed, placing my hand over his mouth. "You need to hide," I whispered.

"What?"

"Cove!" Jace banged on the wood. "Open the door!"

Deacon started walking toward it, but I sharply stepped in front of him.

"He's a chaperone. You have to hide."

"Open the fucking door!"

"Why is he talking to you like that?"

"I promise I'll explain everything to you, but please... you have to hide."

Deacon growled, reluctantly walking out to the balcony. I quickly shut the slider behind him, making sure to close the curtains too.

"Cove!" Jace roared.

I jumped out of my skin, hurrying to unlock the door. "What?!" I screamed, annoyed with him.

It wasn't until Jace's predatory glare raked down my body that I remembered I was only wearing a bra and panties. His greedy stare had me frozen in place.

So he was attracted to me?

"What is it with you and opening the door half fucking naked?"

"I... I..."

In one quick motion, he lifted off his hoodie and covered my body with it. "Put this on. Now!"

I did as I was told, shaking off the spell I was wholeheartedly in with him. Moving past me, he scanned the room. "Who's in here with you?"

"Nobody."

"You expect me to believe that when you're dressed like you're ready to be fucked?"

All the color drained from my face.

He didn't falter, not that I expected him to.

"Where is he, Cove?"

I shrugged, looking away. "I don't know what you're talking about."

"Don't play this game with me, bunny. You won't fucking win."

"Relax, Rambo. I'm by myself."

"Dressed like that?"

"Yeah." I didn't meet his eyes, grabbing my cell phone to turn off the music.

"You're lying."

"I'm not."

"Then look me in the eyes when I'm talking to you."

I didn't. "You're not my father. Stop acting like you are."

"Trust me, if I were, I'd already have you over my knee and begging for mercy."

My thighs clenched.

Of all the things to say, he has to say that?

In one stride, Jace was in my face, grabbing my chin to look at him.

"Where is he? I won't ask you again."

Paying close attention to my mannerisms, I blinked normally, responding, "I already told you, G.I. Joe. I'm by myself."

"The worst fucking thing you can do is lie to me."

"I'm—"

"Don't say I didn't warn you."

He sped around the room, looking under the bed and in the closets.

"Will you stop? No one is in here!"

When his eyes flew to the slider, my heart dropped again. He must have noticed since we both sprinted toward it, but I got there first.

Putting my hands out in front of me, I exclaimed, "What the fuck is your problem? You're acting like you're jealous."

"If you think that's going to work on me, then you don't know me at all."

"You're right. I don't."

"Move, or I'll do it for you."

"I'm not—"

He leaned forward, tossing me over his shoulder with my ass now in his face.

"Jace, quit it!"

He didn't listen, flinging me on the bed. Once he roughly opened the curtains and then slid the doors open, I jumped to my feet. Not knowing what to expect.

"Jace, leave—" I hesitated, realizing Deacon was nowhere to be found. We were up five stories, but that didn't stop me from looking over the railing.

Where did he go?

"Happy now? I told you nobody was here."

I could tell by his pissed-off composure he didn't believe me for a second. It all happened so fast. One minute, we're arguing like cats and dogs, and the next, our eyes both locked on the wallet Deacon left behind under the table. I lunged for it at the same time he did, but I was closer and grabbed it first. Impulsively not thinking, I put the wallet inside my panties. Right on my pussy.

"You think that will stop me?"

I opened my mouth to respond, but in one fluid motion, Jace gripped my wrists and turned me around, pressing my face and the front of my body against the screen door while he held my arms above my head.

I loudly gasped as my chest rapidly rose and fell.

With his other grip on my hip, he pinned me against the slider. I was held hostage in his tight hold.

From behind me, he rasped in my ear, "You have no idea who you're fucking with, bunny."

I didn't know what to say.

I was barely breathing.

His grip on my hip slowly shifted toward my inner thigh as he slid his fingers up my leg, taking the bottom of his hoodie with him.

"What are you doing?"

"Digging for gold."

His callused fingers slid up my stomach before he glided them into my panties, touching the top of my mound. My thighs immediately clenched, feeling my core getting wet. I swallowed hard, melting into his touch. Deacon's hands didn't compare to Jace's. He didn't come close to the way Jace was making me hot all over.

It wasn't until he bit out in a husky tone, "And my little bunny has a completely shaved pussy," that I slightly gasped, surprised by his outburst but also turned on as hell.

"Who would've thought," he added in the same throaty voice.

Does that mean he thinks about me too?

Within seconds, his fingers skimmed my outer lips, and it was over before it even began. He growled as he yanked Deacon's wallet out from my panties, backing away from me.

I felt the loss of his touch instantly.

The moment I turned around to look at him, he was already walking into his room. Never once…

Looking back at me or what he just intentionally put me through.

CHAPTER 9
COVE

The past five and a half weeks were a whirlwind, beginning with graduation two weeks ago. The day replayed in my mind often without me even realizing it.

"Welcome graduates, colleagues, family, and friends. Congratulations to everyone moving forward with their lives today," the principal of our school announced through his microphone, standing front and center on the stage before all of us. *"I'd like to begin by thanking all of the families and friends in the audience this morning. I know how proud you must be of your sons or daughters stepping into the next chapter of their lives. I, myself, have a son who will be graduating next year, and words can't describe the sense of pride I feel for him."*

I couldn't believe the day was finally here. I was no longer in high school, and the future was mine for the taking. I applied to several colleges and got accepted into every last one.

I was foolish to think my parents would be in the audience, proud as fuck for their only child graduating. I'd think, as a parent, it'd be as much of a milestone as it was for their children. I even reminded my mom a few days ago, silently praying they'd pull through for me just this once, but I was hit with the harsh reality they didn't give a shit. They weren't sitting in the stands screaming my name in sheer joy and excitement.

I felt like I was truly abandoned by their selfishness. A monumental moment that was supposed to be about me turned into a day they completely ruined.

Upon receiving my diploma, I tried to stay in the moment, but I couldn't. After I shook everyone's hands on stage, I gazed at the audience, looking for my parents again, thinking maybe I couldn't find them from where I was sitting. Only to be slapped in the face with no one.

As I was walking off the stage, out of nowhere, my disappointed gaze connected with Jace's. The last thing I wanted was for him to psychoanalyze me, so I peered down at the ground instead. To my misfortune, he sat at the end of the row where I had to pass by on my way back to my seat. My classmates were still in front of me, and we were all waiting for the line to move.

I tried my best to ignore him. Since Grad Weekend when I played the role of his assistant, if I didn't have to be around him, I wasn't. When I woke up the next morning, Deacon's wallet was on my nightstand, and we didn't speak about him or what happened the night prior. I knew in the forefront of my mind that if we talked about Deacon, then we'd have to chat about what occurred between us, and I guess it was easier to pretend it didn't happen.

However, I couldn't stop thinking about his hands on me and how he made me feel. Still, Deacon didn't come close to the emotions Jace effortlessly pulled out of me.

The longer I stood there, the more I could feel the tears pooling in my eyes *because my parents were not there for me. Before I moved back to my seat, Jace tugged on my gown, making me peer down at him.*

Through the noise of the families in the stands, he mouthed, "Don't cry, bunny. They're not worth it."

My heart fluttered, smiling at him, but our moment was cut way too short. I had to walk back to my seat. It wasn't until I was almost there that I saw the person I least expected leaning against one of the bleachers at the far end of the auditorium with his arms crossed over his chest.

Deacon.

When I asked him where he escaped that night, he said he slipped onto the balcony next to my room and decided to leave. Stating some shit about it wasn't meant to be for our first time.

Now several weeks later, the guilt of still thinking about Jace was eating away at me, especially after Deacon showed up at my graduation of all places.

"Hey," Deacon chimed, pulling my mind back to the present. "Where did you go?"

"Oh… I was just thinking about graduation."

"You looked beautiful that day."

I smirked. "I still can't believe you were there."

"Where else would I be? I wouldn't have missed it for the world, beauty."

After the ceremony was over, I ran into Deacon's arms. Unfortunately, by the time we worked our way through the crowd, he had to go back to work, so I went with Haven and her family out to lunch like I'd originally planned. They were really sweet. Her father even bought me a stunning diamond cross necklace. It was similar to the one he got for Haven, expressing in his card that I'd always feel like another daughter to him.

It was what I needed to hear. I'd never been more grateful for the Beckhams than I was that morning. Despite hardly saying a word to Jace at lunch, I couldn't help but want to say so much to him, yet I didn't know where to start.

I wish I could tell you I stopped thinking about him.

I wish I could tell you I still hated him.

I wish I could tell you a lot of things that weren't true.

It was like he put a spell on me, etching himself into my head, where he made me think about him all the time. As the weeks continued, my feelings for him did too. Except I barely understood what they meant at this point. It was confusing, to say the least. It didn't help that Deacon had been away on business for the past two and a half weeks, and my best friend was overseas living her best like with her boyfriend.

All I had time to do was think.

Determined to get over whatever bullshit emotions coursed through me when it came to Jace, I devised a plan. Tonight, I surprised Deacon at his house with dinner, wearing a slutty maid uniform I found online. I wouldn't take no for an answer this time.

He was still a gentleman.

Sweet.

Attentive.

Caring.

He was my very own Prince Charming, and I was ready to give him my virginity.

"How about you let me thank you for my lovely dinner and this getup you're wearing for me?" He kissed along my neck up to my lips.

"Oh yeah?" I smirked against his mouth.

"Do you have any idea what you do to me? How much I think about you?"

I beamed, staring up into his eyes.

"Your body is sinful, beauty. That's all I kept thinking about while I was away. How much I wanted to get lost inside you. Instead, I stroked my cock to the vision of you."

My eyes widened, and my breathing hitched.

"I couldn't take my mind off you. You've consumed every last part of me."

He gripped my ass, wrapping my legs around his waist as he carried me toward his bedroom. Easing me onto the mattress, he hovered his muscular body over mine.

Kissing me.

Devouring me.

Making me feel like I was only his.

At first, his kiss was soft, taking my slightly parted lips as an open invitation to slowly slip his tongue into my awaiting mouth. He tasted of scotch and something else I couldn't quite put my finger on. Deepening our kiss, he tightly gripped the back of my neck, and our tongues tangled in urgency and demand.

In one quick movement, he parted my legs with his and set his hard cock right on top of my heat, making me shudder with desire.

"You feel so fucking good, beauty."

His hand skimmed down from my neck to the side of my breast, leaving a trail of longing in his wake. Before I knew it, my maid costume was on the floor, and I was left in just my bra and panties.

He groaned, loud and hard from deep within his chest as his predatory regard consumed my entire being.

His touch.

His scent.

His sounds.

"I love you," he rasped in one breath, tugging the seam of my silk panties down.

The instant I sat up, expressing, "I love you too," all fucking hell broke loose.

It wasn't Deacon's eyes I locked with…

It was the man standing by his bedroom door, wearing a ski mask that captured my attention.

"What the fu—"

He lifted his gun, rendering me speechless at the exact time Deacon turned around to see what startled me.

The minutes turned into hours and the hours into days as my whole life played out in front of me in a matter of seconds. I'd forever remember what happened next like it was a tragic love story.

"What are you—"

BANG!

A loud popping sound ricocheted off the walls from the gunman, and I screamed bloody murder as a sudden warmth sprayed all over my face.

My neck.

My chest.

For a moment, I thought he shot me, but I couldn't have been more wrong when Deacon's body came crashing down on me. All two hundred pounds of him fell lax on top of my petite frame. If I thought I couldn't breathe before, Deacon's blood and brains on my skin undoubtedly proved me wrong.

From that point forward, I was there, but I wasn't.

The sudden weight of Deacon's dead body was thrown off me like he weighed nothing.

"Stop fucking screaming," someone snarled close to my ear, but I could barely hear them.

"Stop fucking fighting me," the man sneered again.

I could barely hear him. My ears were ringing too loudly while the room closed in on me.

He murdered my boyfriend…

It repeated in my mind with no end in sight.

The man gripped my arm, yanking me up to stand on my wobbly legs. I instantly fell over into his solid muscular chest. His arms wrapped around me, holding me close to make sure I wouldn't fall.

"If you know what's good for you," he growled in my ear again. "You'll fucking stop." I could barely see through the haze of blood and God knows what else on my face and body. It all happened so fast I didn't have time to register what occurred next.

The masked man spun me around with my back now to his front, whispering in my ear this time what sounded like, "Fuck around and find out," before he put a rag over my nose and mouth and then…

Everything went black.

CHAPTER 10
COVE

I felt the soft, warm sheets beneath me before I even opened my eyes. My body feeling as if it was one with the mattress. A floating sensation stirred through me. My head was as light as a feather, even though my body felt as heavy as a brick, sinking further and further into the linen sheets.

The smell and sounds of the waves of the ocean immediately assaulted my senses.

Where was I?

I swallowed hard, fully aware there were no beaches in Wyoming. Wherever I was, it was far from home.

"You're finally awake," a distorted male voice announced in the room a few feet away from where I was passed out.

I was instantly terrified, feeling fear in a way I never had.

How much time has passed? What is he going to do with me now that I'm awake? Will he kill me too?

No, or he would have already, right?

Question after question flew through my mind at rapid speed. One wouldn't end before the next one began.

My eyes fluttered open, or maybe they were still closed. The room I was apparently passed out in was pitch black which was why my sounds and smells were heightened in the first place. I couldn't see an inch in front of me as I quickly freaked the fuck out internally.

I didn't say a word or make a peep; I hadn't even moved yet. Too scared of what would happen when I did. I couldn't fathom how he knew I was awake. I barely realized I was awake. Before I could finish that thought, the night's disturbing events came crashing down on me like a pile of bricks. What was supposed to be one of the most memorable nights of my life turned into one of the most traumatic.

All I heard next was the sound of a switch clicking on the nightstand. The light immediately blinded me, illuminating the bedroom. My heart pounded against my chest, my mind once again reeling with thoughts of why I was there, and what he was going to do with me next. I wanted to look around the room, but I couldn't will myself to look away from him. If I peered around the room, it'd make it too real. My subconscious was protecting me from the reality of what had become my life.

Our gazes locked with my emotions running wild inside me.

Every last fiber of my being screamed at me to ask him all the questions tearing apart my brain, but I knew I wouldn't get any answers. However, it didn't stop me from wanting to ask them anyway.

I opened my mouth to say something, anything, when he interrupted, reading my mind, "You want answers," through this device he held over his mouth to distort his voice.

I hesitantly nodded, not being able to find my own voice. The feelings stirring through me were crippling me in ways I never thought possible. There was no holding back anymore.

I exploded, bursting into hysterics while my body began shaking uncontrollably.

It was too much.

It was too real.

I was battling the inevitable of losing this unexpected war I found myself in.

"Cove, stop crying."

Shit!

He knew my name, setting off a whole other level of terror, causing me to emotionally breakdown. This was far worse than when Mrs. Beckham died. I thought about the life I still wanted to live and the future I deserved to have with all the people I wouldn't get to see again or say goodbye to.

Would my parents even notice I was gone? Would they care?

"Look at me," he demanded, further freaking me the fuck out.

I fervently shook my head, tightly shutting my eyes.

"I said look at me."

"NO!"

I should have known better, but of course I didn't. My mom always said my defiance would eventually get the best of me, and she wasn't wrong.

"Cove—"

"NO!" I put my hands over my ears, laying my head on my knees and curled into a protective ball as if it would rescue me from this horrible scenario.

The instant I felt his hands yanking my arms away from my ears, my fight-or-flight defenses finally kicked in, and I chose fight. I fought with everything inside me, knowing my life depended on it.

Kicking.

Punching.

Screaming.

I laid it all out, finding strength I didn't know I had in me.

Until he pinned my body onto the bed, holding my wrists above my head. Now he was hovering above me, making me much more vulnerable in this position with him on top of me than I was before. I was at his mercy, and he knew it too.

Still, I didn't open my eyes. Scared of the consequences of what I just did and what would happen because I didn't listen.

Suddenly, his cell phone rang, and he loosened his hold for a second. Thinking quick on my feet, I opened my eyes to find him reaching for it. I used his moment of distraction to my advantage and kneed him in the balls as hard as I could, silently thanking Reid for teaching me this self-defense technique.

He groaned, falling forward but before he could fall onto the bed, I shoved his body off me and hauled fucking ass. His body collapsed to the floor in a loud, hard thud, and I instantly felt an immense sense of satisfaction that I could at least hurt him.

Ignoring the unsteadiness of my body and mind, I rushed out of the room and slammed the door behind me. I grabbed the chair beside the frame, setting it under the doorknob, securing it in place in hopes of locking him in there to give me time to escape.

With one foot in front of the other, I tore through the place I was being held captive in. I ran as fast as I could down the narrow hallway, my bare feet mercilessly pounding on the floor. It was only then I noticed I was cleaned up, wearing a man's shirt and boxers, but naked underneath it.

Did he undress me? Wash me? What else happened while I was passed out?

Trying to stay focused on the present, I sped through the house at rapid speed, looking for a front door or anywhere else I could escape from.

Hide.

Pray.

Wait for my rescue…

Someone would find me, right? Someone would be looking for me? Haven? Her family? Maybe even Jace?

"Help!" I shouted, banging on the walls. "Somebody please help me!"

I ran as fast as I could through another vaguely lit hallway, only stopping to check the few doors that lined the walls to see if they were open. Trying the handles, I pounded my fists for some sort of miracle that one would open.

They were all locked, and I couldn't help but contemplate if other women were in them.

Was I being trafficked? Sold to the highest bidder? Didn't they usually pay more for a virgin?

Deacon… how I wish you were still with me.

"Help! PLEASE! SOMEBODY PLEASE HELP ME!"

I heard the door to the room I was being held in kicked down. It echoed through the walls and into the core of my being. The sound of his shoes dragged on the wooden floors. He was coming for me, that much I knew was true. Terror set in again, and I took off running, looking back to make sure he wasn't behind me, not paying attention to where I was going.

Frantically, I tried to catch my bearings while I looked around needing to find something I could use as a weapon.

Nothing.

Not one damn thing.

Instead, I hid under the clothed table with my back against the wall. My heart was hammering out of my chest. It was so loud I swear he could hear it. Placing my hand over my mouth, I concentrated on softly breathing through my nose like a masked man wasn't chasing after me.

I watched through the slits of my eyes as his steps passed by my body, but at the last second, he abruptly turned and gripped my ankles, triggering me to scream and kick to no avail until he once again pinned me to the ground beneath him.

I tightly shut my eyes, moving my head side to side, refusing to look at him. In a hard, demanding grip, he grabbed my chin, making me face him. Because I was a defiant woman, it was in my nature and part of my DNA at this point. My eyes snapped open, and I impulsively spit in his face, landing right on his lips.

To my complete horror, he slowly licked his mouth from one end to the other, cocking his head to the side as if he was baiting me.

Jace's warning from the night he carried me out of the bar crept through my brain.

"One day you're going to find yourself in a lot of trouble if you don't start changing your ways."

He was right.

Fuck!

Unable to help myself, I spewed, "Why are you still wearing a mask? Huh? Why are you using a voice machine? You have the balls to kill my boyfriend and take me captive, but not the balls to show me who you really are? You know what that proves to me? You're nothing but a fucking pussy!"

For good measure, I spit in his face again. Except this time, it landed right near his eye. I wasn't expecting him to scoff out a chuckle, obviously amused with my outburst.

Still feeling feisty, I pushed more boundaries, adding, "People will look for me. As a matter of fact, my best friend's brother is retired military and a fucking badass! He'll find me, and when he does, he'll fucking kill you!"

M. Robinson

I don't know why I used Jace as my hero. Maybe it was just hopeful thinking or perhaps it was just me being a blatant idiot.

He snidely grinned as he grabbed the edge of his ski mask.

I laid there on pins and needles, waiting for the inevitable. Once I saw him, there was no going back, I'd be an eyewitness if they found me.

But when would that be?

Despite the harsh outcome of seeing his face, it didn't stop my desire to see who he was.

In one swift movement, he showed me the man behind the facade.

"Oh my God."

I just never expected him to reveal...

Jace fucking Beckham was now the villain instead of my hero.

CHAPTER 11
JACE

H er bright-blue eyes widened as she lay there in disbelief.

I was the first to break the deafening silence between us, stating, "I'll back off, but only if you promise not to fight me anymore."

Completely in shock, she thought about it for a second before slowly nodding.

I released her wrists and then hesitantly started moving away with my hands out in front of me in a gesture of surrender. As soon as I was sitting on the balls of my boots, she tried to punch me in the face, but I caught it mid strike, which only further pissed her off. I couldn't blame her. If anything, I was proud as fuck of the courage she held in such a life-and-death situation.

Cove was a lot stronger than I ever gave her credit for, and that was saying something, considering I thought she was already pretty brave for all the shit her parents put her through.

Not letting up, she began fighting me again, but I was at my wits' end with her to begin with.

"Calm down," I ordered, blocking her attacks.

"Calm down?! You want me to calm down?! You killed my boyfriend, you fucking asshole! I loved him, and he's the only man who's ever loved me!"

"That's it!" I loudly growled. "I'm over this shit!" I stood, dragging her with me.

"Jace, don't you—"

I threw her over my shoulder, carrying her back to the bedroom of the safe house we were in.

She kicked and screamed the whole way, putting up one hell of a fight. However, I didn't expect anything less from her at this point.

"Jace! Put me down!"

I did, slamming her ass onto the bed. Before she could give me more shit, I grabbed the handcuffs from my back pocket, cuffing one of her wrists to the iron rod on the headboard.

She jerked back when she realized what I just did.

"No!" Yanking her hand back, she tried to break free.

"Stop, or you're going to hurt yourself."

She glared at me. "Not any more than you already have!"

Inhaling a deep breath, I desperately tried to keep my cool although I was on the brink of insanity when it came to her.

"What the hell is going on?!"

"The less you know, the better."

"What kind of bullshit response is that?"

"The only one I'm giving you."

We were at a standoff for a moment before I opened the curtains, letting some natural light in. Once she noticed we were on a secluded island, her eyebrows pinched together.

"Where am I?"

"Where I want you to be."

"Which is where?"

Grabbing the armchair, I slid it beside her and sat down. Leaning forward, I set my elbows on my knees, contemplating what I would say to her next.

Her long blond hair flowed all around her face and down the sides of her body. Her complexion was pale, and her pouty lips were dry from dehydration. Taking her in for a second, I nodded to the glass of water on the nightstand.

In true Cove rebellion, she knocked it off with the back of her hand, and it crashed at my feet, shattering to the floor all around me.

"Bunny..." I warned in a tense tone.

"Don't bunny me, asshole! Why would you keep scaring me like this if it was you all along under that ski mask?"

"I was trying to make it easier on you by seeing me as the bad guy and not your fucking hero."

"I was only saying that because—"

"No need to bullshit me. I know why you were."

"Oh, that's right! I forgot you know everything about me."

"You think this is easy for me, Cove? You're my little sister's best fucking friend!"

She quickly grimaced. "You were never going to show me your face?"

"I was, on my time, not yours, but you made it completely fucking impossible for me not to reveal myself!"

"Don't yell at me! How about you think for one minute what I'm going through, you selfish son of a bitch?!"

I growled as my hands fisted at my sides. "All I've done is think about you. If I hadn't, you'd be dead already!"

I spent the past few hours sitting in this goddamn chair, waiting for her to wake up. After I chloroformed her, I carried her body back to my vehicle and drove us the hell out of there while making sure nobody followed us. About an hour later, she was lying on the seat in the back of a private jet I was flying for the next seven hours with only one stop to refuel.

I had to inject her with a powerful sedative to keep her asleep the entire time, but I didn't leave her side for a second. By the time we got back to this safe house in the middle of nowhere, I laid her in the tub.

I fucking hated seeing that motherfucker's blood and remnants of his brain and skull tainting her skin. Gently, I wiped off his dried blood from her face and body, cutting off her bra and panties with my knife next, exposing her bare flesh. I bathed her as best I could, given our shitty circumstances.

After I cleaned her up, I grabbed my shirt and boxers from my bag and dressed her in them. She drowned in my clothes. As I carried her to the bed, she didn't stir once, and we hadn't moved since. I watched her all night, waiting for her to wake up. I was used to not sleeping. Surviving on only an hour or two for weeks at a time was how I operated.

"Are you just going to sit there and be all you?" She gestured her hand toward me, working it up and down.

"This is how it's going to go down, bunny. You're not going to ask any more questions—"

"The hell I'm not!"

"If you interrupt me one more fucking time, I'll gag you. Do you understand me? Nod your pretty little head if you do."

I could see it in her eyes. She wanted to defy me. However, she reluctantly nodded instead.

"Good girl."

Her jaw clenched.

"Trust me, Cove. I know this is really hard for you, but you have two choices here. You can either listen to every order I give you or..." I paused, letting my words sink in. "You can die."

She opened her mouth but quickly remembered my warning.

"Good girl."

She scowled at me, mouthing, "Please."

I sighed, unwillingly giving in to her. "Ask."

She didn't hesitate. "This is bullshit! You break into Deacon's home and murder him in cold blood, and now I'm just expected to trust you when you kill my boyfriend for what? What the hell is going on?"

I didn't waver in my reaction. "Deacon wasn't who you thought he was."

She narrowed her eyes at me.

"And neither am I."

"I don't understand."

"And you're not going to."

"Try me. Please. I need to know you're not going to hurt me."

"For now, you're safe with me."

"For now?"

"Do you want to live, Cove?"

"Of course."

"Then you're going to have to trust me."

"Trust the asshole who murdered the man I love?"

"You didn't love him, bunny."

"Don't you dare tell me how I felt about Deacon, Jace."

"You loved the man you thought he was. The one he pretended to be to make you fall for his bullshit. You were just a target to get to me."

She jerked back. "To you?"

"Everything from the moment you met him in the gas station has been a lie. Starting with his name, to his age, to where the fuck he lived. Nothing of the man you thought you knew—"

"That's not true!"

"You can't be this naive."

She winced, not trying to hide it from me. "So he was just using me?"

I shrugged. "You made it easy for him to."

Her eyes widened in disbelief. It was blatantly obvious that her mind was spinning out of control. The realization of my statement caused her more turmoil than it did ease.

She peered around the room, avoiding my eyes. Her emotions were getting the best of her.

"I want to go home," she whispered so low.

"You're not safe there anymore. You need to be here."

She frowned, tears pooling in her eyes as she bowed her head, defeated. "With you?"

"Yes. With me, bunny."

"You promise you won't hurt me?"

Unable to avoid it, I instinctively demanded, "Look me in the eyes when I'm talking to you," as if she was just another hostage I was interrogating.

She peered up at me through her long, dark lashes as a few tears streamed down the sides of her face, but she instantly wiped them away, not wanting me to see her looking so weak.

Still, she didn't understand I could read her like the back of my hand without even trying.

"You're safe here for the time being," I answered her question the best I could. "Deacon wasn't who you thought he was. You can't go home because now you're in danger from men like him."

"Men like you too?"

"Something like that."

She gave me a questioning stare. "What about you?"

"What about me?"

"Are you in danger too?"

"Bunny, I'm always in fucking danger. It comes with the territory of who I am and what I'm trained to do."

It hurt her to hear the truth out of my mouth. I could tell she felt bad for me, and I'd be lying if I said it didn't faze me.

It did.

Much more than I cared to admit.

I couldn't remember the last time someone did.

"Did you know Deacon or whatever his name was?"

"It doesn't matter."

"It does to me."

"I suggest the next time you fall in love with a man—"

"I thought... I just thought... I mean... I've never had a boyfriend before him, and I thought... he loved me." Her eyes rimmed with fresh tears. "I finally found someone who did."

I blew off her response, refusing to let it sink in. Knowing exactly why she felt the need to share that with me. I couldn't help but notice how tiny and vulnerable she appeared. How exposed she was to me at that moment.

For a woman who hid behind her strength, it was hard to watch. At least it was...

For me.

She slowly licked her lips, trying to govern her unsteady breathing. Hoping I didn't realize how much she wanted me to touch her.

Hold her.

Comfort her.

I didn't.

I couldn't.

I wasn't made like that.

"None of this makes any sense to me."

"The more questions you ask, the less it's going to."

"If he's a liar, then what are you?"

"Right now, I'm Jace Beckham. Your best friend's older brother."

"Right now?" she coaxed, meeting my eyes. "What does that mean?"

"It means in a few short hours, I'll need you to be someone else too. If you want to stay alive, you'll have to follow my rules."

She shook her head. "I thought you were retired military?"

"I am."

"Does your family know—"

"Anyone who knows what I do becomes a target, Cove. In order to keep my family safe, they think I'm just retired military now."

"So what do you do, Jace?"

"Bunny—"

"I'm already a target, according to you. I have nothing left to lose. You want me to trust you? Then you're going to have to tell me the truth. Who are you, G.I. Joe?"

I wanted to provide her the only security I could, which only put her life in more danger, and trust me, the irony was not lost on me. Despite feeling uneasy about telling her who I was, I answered her persistent question as if I was a man on death row, and in some cases, I was. This was one of them.

Looking deep into her eyes, I shared the truth of my identity for the first time…

"I'm a contract killer, Cove."

CHAPTER 12
JACE
THEN: TONY'S FUNERAL

He was gone.

Forever.

Never coming back.

I watched from the door of their bedroom as Hope, his now widowed fiancée, stared at her black dress on their bed that I knew she bought for his funeral. She told me yesterday morning she wanted something she could throw away after wearing it. Something she would never have to look at again.

I'd been staying in their guest bedroom since I landed late the night prior. I only had a three-day leave of absence to present his family with his dog tags and flag at his service that afternoon. His wake was scheduled for that morning.

She'd been staring at it for the last hour, dreading to put it on. I knew because I also dreaded wearing my crisp, white Navy SEAL dress uniform. This was all happening. We were preparing to say goodbye to a man we both loved.

For the second time in what felt as if it were simply a couple of minutes, I wore my dress uniform for a funeral for yet another person who was like family to me.

In the blink of an eye, everything that happened in the last couple of days flew by at rapid speed through my mind. I had no control over it, which was the worst thing for a man like me.

"You don't have to wear that, Hope," I announced, leaning against the doorframe with my hands in the pockets of my slacks.

She turned with her tear-stricken face, staring right at me. Almost like she could see inside me, and we were one and the same.

"You can wear whatever you want. Tony would want it that way."

She shook her head. "I don't think I can put anything on. It doesn't matter what it is or how it looks or feels. Ultimately, I know what it's for, so it doesn't change anything," she whispered so low I could barely hear her.

She looked at me with an expression I also knew far too well. Tony was like another brother to me.

But I couldn't protect him.

Save him.

He died because of me.

"I'll help you get through this day," I coaxed, walking toward her.

She was in shock.

Disoriented.

Grief was one hell of an emotion.

I tried to focus on all the times we were together. I knew Hope through him, and since he talked about her often, she felt like family to me too.

Once I stood in front of her, I placed my hand on her shoulder, gently squeezing in reassurance.

"I'm so sorry, Hope."

"I don't think I can do this, Jace."

"You can, and you will. Let me help you."

Doing what I had to do, I grabbed her black dress off the hanger and told her to lift her arms, so I could gently ease it down her body before helping her with her shoes next. Nothing about what I was doing was sexual. I was merely helping his fiancée's distress for a day filled of pure agony and regret.

After I helped her get ready, I stood in front of her and swept her hair from her face.

"You look beautiful, Hope."

"I don't feel beautiful."

When we heard her mother yell for us, I grabbed her hand, murmuring all sorts of reassuring things to her.

"What's going to happen now?"

"We're going to say goodbye to Tony."

"What about our baby? I don't have a job—"

"I promised Tony I'd take care of the both of you, okay? Don't worry about anything. I'm here for you."

She faintly nodded. "Okay."

During the funeral, I stood in a trance-like state for the service until it was time to do my duty to the best friend I'd ever known.

Handing Hope the flag, I expressed, "On behalf of the president of the United States, the United States Navy, and a grateful nation, please accept this flag as a symbol of our appreciation for your loved one's honorable and faithful service."

She broke down, and I swear I felt two feet tall instead of six-four. There was nothing but an empty feeling deep in whatever remained of my soul.

After the funeral was over, I stayed there, watching as they shoveled dirt onto Tony's new home. For the rest of the day, I didn't move an inch from his grave until nothing but darkness surrounded me, making me feel like I died as well.

It could have been a handful of minutes, a few hours, or a couple of days that passed in front of my eyes. Time didn't seem to matter while I was frozen in place.

In time.

I tried to find a bit of peace, even though I didn't deserve it.

I allowed my mind and body to seek shelter in that dark place within me, and I was starting to think I'd never come out into the light again. This was simply my penance for taking another life that didn't belong to me.

I inhaled a deep, sturdy breath, breathing in through my nose and out through my mouth before I confessed to him, "I don't remember what it feels like to have a good night's rest. Sometimes it's well into the morning before my eyes finally close, and exhaustion takes over. It's never peaceful sleep, though. My mind refuses to shut off even though I'm mentally spent from the wheels turning at full speed all hours of the day. The guilt festering inside me is eating me alive, Tony. I keep thinking about the what-ifs, but they don't matter because they won't bring you or my mother back. At times, it feels like I'm lost without her. Other times it feels like I was lost long before I didn't get to say goodbye to her." I hesitated for a moment.

"I'm so fucking sorry, man. I hope you know that. I pray that your soul finally rests in peace, but in the back of my mind, I know we don't deserve peace for all the lives we've claimed in the past eleven years. I feel my mother's presence everywhere I go, and I know I don't deserve it, yet there she is, always with me. Even as I claimed your life, she watched me raise that gun with nothing but shame and sadness in her eyes." I swallowed hard, holding in the tears and guilt suffocating me for killing my best friend.

"I'm just trying to put the pieces of my life back together, but it's so fucking hard when I lose myself more as the days go on. I'm so sorry. This is all my fault. You shouldn't have lost your life protecting mine. I hope you know that too. I hope you believe it. I hope you're happy and at peace. I hope so many fucking things for you." An unexpected shiver ran down my spine from the sudden breeze. Almost like he was making his presence known. He was there for me, comforting me the only way he could now.

"I fucking love you, man," I whispered into the misty air. "I don't know who I am anymore and maybe I never did. I struggle with everything these days. You'd be so disappointed in me, or maybe you already are. I don't know." I shook my head. "I don't know anything anymore. Everything hurts right now. I don't know what it feels like not to hurt. The pain is a part of me, and I feel like I'm dying all the time. A little bit of my air is being taken from my lungs each day, enough to know it's missing. It's leaving me, and I can't do anything to save it, knowing it's happening, and I can't stop it. All I can do is wait for the day when I can't breathe any longer. How do I forget about all the shit we've done?"

With a solemn expression, I threw dirt on his grave before confessing my last truth...

"I wish it were me that was dead and not you."

CHAPTER 13
COVE

"**H**ow long do you plan on keeping me handcuffed to this bed?"

"As long as it takes to know I can trust my balls around you."

I resisted the urge to smile. "Well, you should have known better about who you kidnapped, Mr. Know-It-All."

He nodded at me. "Who taught you how to defend yourself like that?"

"You can thank your brother Reid for that one."

"Reid, huh?"

"Yeah, he taught Haven and me some moves when we started growing boobs."

He scoffed out a chuckle. "What else did he teach you?"

"All your brothers have taught Haven and me something."

"Care to elaborate?"

"Well… Ledger taught us how to ride a horse."

"He was basically born on one."

"He's the one that's inheriting the ranch, right?"

"That's what I'm told."

"You don't want it?"

"I have no interest in cow shit for the rest of my life."

"Oh, but killing people for the rest of your life seems normal?"

He ignored my question. "Since Reid taught you how to fight. Where does that leave Alexander and Troy?"

"Alexander taught us that all guys wanted from us was to get laid."

"That sounds about right."

"He also said that if we had sex with a boy before we got married, he'd end up in jail, but that was only after we were old enough to realize that kissing and holding hands doesn't get us pregnant like he claimed."

He scoffed out another chuckle.

"Troy taught us how to do a keg stand and to lie without smiling."

He muttered under his breath. "He's more lost than I am."

I arched an eyebrow, taking in what he just shared. I wanted to call him out on it. However, I decided it wasn't the right time to get him to open up to me more than he already had.

The fact that I still thought I could get him to confide in me even after everything he put me through wasn't lost on me.

Instead of continuing our conversation, I pointed out the obvious. "Don't think I don't know what you're doing, Jace."

He cocked his head to the side, baiting me.

"You're not the only one who knows things. I know some things too."

"Enlighten me."

"You mean how you're trying to establish a connection with me, so I'll trust you and follow all your orders like a good girl."

He grinned, not trying to hide it. "Is it working?"

"No," I adamantly replied.

"No?" he taunted.

"What do you want from me?"

"Now that's a loaded question if I've ever heard one, bunny."

My stomach fluttered.

What did he mean by that?

"You still haven't answered my question."

He narrowed his gaze at me.

"What?"

"I didn't say anything."

"You didn't have to. It's written all over your face."

"And what's my face telling you, Cove?"

"That I'm not going to like whatever you're about to order me to do."

"You may like it."

It was my turn to narrow my eyes at him.

He nodded to the nightstand next to me. "Open the drawer."

"Why?"

"I didn't ask for a question."

"You know this whole controlling thing you have." I gestured to him. "You really need to work on that."

"Open the drawer, bunny. I hate repeating myself, and I won't do it again."

"You could at least say please," I mumbled before following his command, going against my nature.

As soon as I saw the red velvet jewelry box, I jerked back in confusion. "What is that?"

"Open it and find out."

With a shaky breath, I reached inside and grabbed it. Never once imagining what happened next.

When I opened the box, Jace declared as if it were nothing, "You're now my wife, bunny. Whether you want to be or not."

Jace

"Okay," she snapped in an overwhelmed tone. "I can't take it anymore. Just stop talking for a minute."

I waited, allowing her a moment to let it sink in, and she burst into tears the second it did.

I never handled women crying very well.

Motherfucker.

"Bunny, I need you to be strong for me. You can't break down like this. You have to be brave."

"That's your pep talk?" she bellowed, wiping her tears. "You're fucking fired."

"I know this is hard for you."

"You keep saying that, but you don't mean it."

"Cove, I'm hanging on by an extremely thin thread. I don't have the time or the patience to deal with your emotional meltdowns every time your hormonal shit takes the wheel."

"You just don't get it…"

"You're right, I don't, and I'm not going to pretend to in order to spare your feelings."

"What happened to you to make you this way? Your mom would be so disappointed in you."

Unfazed, I replied, "You're right again, bunny."

We locked eyes for a second, and I could physically feel her turmoil bleeding into me, becoming part of my skin. She was just another soul I was destroying.

"How am I your wife? I'm supposed to remember getting married, Jace."

"I never said anything about marriage."

That must have been her last straw because my feisty girl made herself known again, spewing, "I don't know how much you know about being someone's wife, but it usually starts with a man getting down on one knee, saying all sort of beautiful things like, 'You're the one. You complete me. I can't live without you,' you know, words of love and devotion."

"Your future husband sounds like a complete pussy."

"You wouldn't know anything about romance if it bit you in the ass and said hello."

"Don't get it twisted. This isn't real. I don't need to marry you for you to be my wife on this mission."

"Mission?"

"Either we're newlyweds on our honeymoon while I try to figure out the mess you've involved yourself in or I have no choice but to—"

"Kill me? Why?"

"You know too much."

"I don't know anything! I don't even know Deacon's real name! You could kill me that easily? You know what? I call your bluff, asshole. I'm your sister's best friend. Even your mom loved me, and your dad said he sees me like another daughter, so try again."

Matching her snide tone, I bit out, "Don't fuck with me, Cove. You know me less than the man you were about to give your virginity to."

She thought about it. "I thought you said I was safe and could trust you?"

"You are if you follow my rules."

"I don't understand."

"You don't need to."

"This is bullshit!"

"No shit! I don't like any of this, but it's the only way I can keep you safe while I try to figure out who's after me."

"How do you even know someone is after me, though?"

"I just do."

"How?"

"What part of me not answering to you do you not understand?"

"I'm just saying. What if you're wrong? What if no one is after me? What if—"

I abruptly stood, roaring, "Because I already received orders to kill you! This isn't a game! I had to put my ass on the line for you, Cove! Why do you think that ring is in there in the first place? This has all been planned out. So either you start marching in line or I'm going to have to put a bullet in your head. Am I making myself fucking clear?"

With a terrified expression, she rasped, "For how long?"

"Don't worry about it."

"Please, Jace. Just tell me how long I have to pretend to love you?"

"Love has nothing to do with this."

She bowed her head, wiping away fresh tears from her eyes.

For the first time in I don't know how long, I craved to comfort her but resisted the desire to handle her with care. It was such a foreign response for me. Cove was triggering a side of me I thought died long ago. It was both a blessing and a curse. I didn't deserve to feel her pain. Not when I was the one inflicting it.

Once again going against my better judgment, I answered her question, "A week."

She scoffed out, "A week or I'm dead."

I grabbed her face to look at me, making sure she comprehended the severity of the situation before I brutally added another truth, "I don't want to kill you, but don't think for a second I'm your fucking hero. Now if you want to make it out this alive, you're going to have to follow my orders, or I'll have no choice but to end you. And trust me, Cove. You'll want me to be the man who does it, not the men who'll silence you for whatever you may or may not know."

Fuck!

This wasn't supposed to happen. She wasn't supposed to be here with me, handcuffed to this goddamn bed like we were playing house in a fucked-up story.

This was bad.

The blaze in her eyes.

The feel of her skin.

The smell of her scent all around

I was fucked.

But it didn't matter. I was already going straight to hell. I just didn't want to drag her there with me.

My expression was impassive, neutral. She couldn't read one damn thing about me, and it further fueled her fire until I let her go and backed away.

Meeting my eyes, she asked, "If I agree to this, what happens next?"

In one breath, I spoke with conviction...

"You're going to have to get used to my touch."

CHAPTER 14
COVE

J ace opened the closest in the room, nodding to the tight, sleek, white, silk dress among the clothes I assumed were hanging for me.

"You have an hour to get ready."

I opened my mouth, but quickly shut it.

"Good girl," he praised, grabbing the dress and throwing it on the bed.

The front of it was cut in a low v, and it looked like it was backless with a high slit on each side of the dress.

"I don't have—"

"Everything you need to get ready is in the bathroom behind that door." He gestured to the corner of the room.

I swallowed hard, suddenly my heart was hammering in my chest for a whole set of different reasons.

I went to speak, but he interrupted, "From this point forward, no more questions, bunny. For the next week, all I expect from you is obedience. Am I making myself clear?"

I simply nodded, fighting with the desire to argue with him.

"Does that mean you're going to unhandcuff me?"

In three calculated strides, he set me free then warned, "Don't make me regret this."

"This isn't a game! I had to put my ass on the line for you, Cove!"

Even with him standing there in front of me, his statement repeated in my mind. I felt like I had no choice in the matter. I had to follow his orders, or I was dead.

In the end, my life was all that mattered.

Surrendering, I promised, "You won't."

With that, he turned and left, closing the door behind him. For a second, I thought he was putting a lot of faith in me until I heard him lock the door from the outside.

"So much for trust…"

I basically moved in autopilot, showering and then applying my makeup before I got dressed. Jace wasn't lying, everything I needed was already there for me, and I couldn't help but wonder how long this had all been planned out.

Whoever prepared my stuff certainly knew my sizes, from the dress to the panties, to stiletto red heels on my feet. The toiletries in the bathroom were some of my favorite products. I couldn't believe how much of what was there, were actually new products of what I'd been using for years.

The hair supplies.

The makeup.

Down to the hairbrush on the sink.

I couldn't shake the eerie feeling of being watched for God knows how long. I wanted to cry and fall apart again, but it was pointless. This was now my life, and I had to embrace it, but it was still so surreal to be in a life-and-death situation. I kept praying this was a nightmare I'd soon wake up from. However, it wasn't.

This was my new reality.

I was nothing more than a target to play with.

A toy.

Exactly how my parents and Deacon, or whatever his name was, treated me.

The longer I was in there by myself, the more I thought about how foolish I'd been in believing what we had was real. I thought he loved me, and that was a massive hit to my self-esteem and dignity.

I truly was just a naive girl looking for love in all the wrong places.

How did I not see through his façade? How could I have been so fucking stupid?

He was such a good actor, and I believed everything he told me.

Hook.

Line.

And sinker.

Once I was done changing, I walked back into the bedroom to find Jace wearing a black tuxedo. Looking like he just stepped out of a James Bond movie. Despite hating him, I couldn't help but be attracted to him.

He was devastatingly handsome.

His dirty-blond hair was pulled back, only emphasizing his bright-blue eyes that felt as if they were staring into my soul. His beard that had a little gray in it merely added to his sex appeal.

This man was twenty years older than me, he could literally be my father, but you wouldn't think that with how my body responded to his intoxicating presence and demeanor.

Jace Beckham was sexy as sin.

I wish I could tell you he was gazing at me with the same infatuation, except he wasn't. The expression on his face showed me nothing. Not one damn thing and I despised that more than anything. Tears of anger burned in my eyes as bile rose in the back of my throat, loathing how he had the power to make me feel so much without even trying.

"Come here," he ordered in that voice I detested.

With one foot in front of the other, I walked toward him until I was standing right in front of him.

"Good girl."

Two words that should have triggered more disgust, started stirring this satisfaction deep inside me and the bastard knew it too. The truth was, Jace could read me like a fucking book.

When did that start happening? How long could he see through me?

"Turn around," he demanded next.

I gave him a questioning glare before I did what he wanted.

"Relax, bunny," he rasped into my ear as he wrapped what felt like a necklace around my neck.

The overwhelming emotions welled up inside me, threatening to spill out as I caught my reflection in the floor-length closet mirror. Right on cue, I watched as Jace attached a chain to the gold collared necklace he just wrapped around my neck.

Wait a second…

I wouldn't cry.

I couldn't.

Because I was suddenly this pet…

He just leashed and collared.

Jace

I never thought I'd be leading my little sister's best friend into such a dangerous and seedy world, but this night would be the ultimate test on whether she'd be able to pull this off.

We'd both be playing a role this evening. Except I was the only professional who knew what they were doing. She looked fucking gorgeous dressed like the vixen I wanted her to appear to be, but I kept my mouth shut. I couldn't give her any compliments she deserved to hear. I'd only confuse her more than she already was if that were even possible at this point.

She stared out the tinted window of the chauffeured SUV driving us to the event. I knew her mind was racing with endless questions, one right after the other. I felt every last one of them coursing through my veins like I was the one thinking them instead.

Unable to continue this way, I demanded, "Ask me, Cove."

She glanced over at me. "Where are we?"

"Saint Martin."

"Well that explains the beaches." She hesitated for a moment. "Can I ask one more question?"

"If you must."

"Where are we going?"

"To a party."

Her eyebrows pinched together as I added, "No more questions."

Twenty minutes later, we pulled up to a port, and I handed her a black, lace bunny masquerade mask.

"What—"

"Put this on."

When she realized what it was, she acknowledged, "A bunny?" with wide eyes.

I ignored her remark. "Unless I tell you otherwise, you speak to no one tonight. Understood?"

Fear crept through her face, and I gave her some reassurance.

"I'll never leave your side."

She immediately let out a visibly relieved breath.

After I put on my mask, I grabbed her hand and led her toward the boat waiting for us at the end of the dock. The ride to the secluded mansion on a private island was invite-only. You couldn't get to this estate without one. The only access to the property was on this boat they provided.

It wasn't the first time I attended one these events, but it was the first time I was attending with a woman I was supposedly married to, nonetheless. Once we arrived at the dock on the estate, I grabbed Cove's leash, and guided her through the island up to the front door.

The guard at the entrance cleared our invites before lifting the red velvet rope and allowing us inside.

The manor was packed with people, making it hard for us to even get by without having to wait a few seconds for the crowds to separate. The farther I led us into the party, the worse our surroundings became. The music pounded through the speakers, vibrating to my core as I tried to make our way over to the back doors.

The place was obviously exceeding capacity, filled to the brim. Everyone was dressed to the nines. Beautiful people just getting their night started, moving to the beat of the music blaring above the crowds. It was quite a presentation—everything from the flashing lights to the neon strobes, strumming around every corner. There were plush couches along the perimeter with tables stacked with open bottles of champagne and liquor while drugs flowed through their obviously fucked-up bodies.

I had no interest in participating in this part of the party.

I didn't give a fuck about any of it. I was only there for one thing, and we'd yet to arrive to our final destination. This wasn't the main event. This was just a cover-up for what was behind door number two and possibly three and four. My enemies needed to know I was there. It was all a show.

Especially for what was still to come.

I proceeded on our descent, and I didn't have to turn around to be aware that Cove was taking it all in as if she was Alice in Wonderland, following the rabbit down the hole.

A long, narrow hallway was nearly pitch black, leading to another door. Another dimension.

Another fucking world.

As soon as the double doors opened, I swear I could feel the demons oozing out, hovering around us. Waiting to drag us under. They called this place Sin. The rules were anything goes.

Sex.

Drugs.

Fucking murder—these black walls had seen it all.

This was where the elite partied since they could get away with anything.

You name it, it was there.

Anonymity was the key purpose of this party. From the second we passed the threshold into Sin it was Sodom and Gomorrah.

Cove loudly gasped, realizing I'd just led her into…

A BDSM sex club.

CHAPTER 15
COVE

A shudder ran through me. I was fully aware Jace was testing my restraint. I'd never seen anything like this in my entire life, looking around the opulent room of women walking, barely dressed in lingerie. In the grand scheme of things, I was dressed pretty modestly compared to them.

Some of the people were on leashes like I was. Others were by themselves, searching for pleasure, pain; what the hell did I know? I had no experience in this environment, yet still I was utterly captivated by it.

What would happen next? Where were we going? What would I see?

Question after question once again plagued my mind on an endless stream of what the fuck was happening. The woman who was on a cross grabbed my attention first. She was being whipped by a man with what appeared to be some sort of leather whip. There were tassels on the end of them, and every time it hit her sensitive flesh, she loudly moaned, getting off on it.

I'd never seen anything like it before, but I wasn't completely naive. I knew places like this existed, yet I never thought I'd be in one. To be there with my best friend's older brother wasn't anything I could have ever predicted. It wasn't entirely terrible, though. If anything, it was the opposite.

Something about being there with Jace Beckham had my thighs clenching with each stride I stepped. Jace strode around as if he owned the damn place. The confidence he exuded, and the way women couldn't take their greedy stares off him wasn't lost on me.

The sad part was, I was jealous of the way they were eyeing him with no shame. They were blatant about it. Jace didn't seem bothered by how both men and women stared at me. He was indifferent toward the whole thing almost like this was normal for him. Which only made me consider how many times he'd attended an event like this and what he participated in.

Was this his lifestyle? Did he whip women too?

My attention shifted toward the women on their knees as their significant other talked to the people around them as if she wasn't there waiting on his next command like a dog.

There was so much I wanted to say.

To scream.

To know…

Translucent lighting was everywhere. Half-naked women danced on poles set up in several places around the open room, food laid on the bare skin of women and men, and servers walked around topless wearing nothing but G-strings. However, everyone was wearing a mask, so you couldn't see their faces.

Simply making the environment that much more intoxicating.

The temptation was out in the open, but behind the masks it didn't make that seedy. People were giving in to their desires, playing a part without having to worry about the repercussions.

Jace sensed my apprehension and curiosity, leading me into a theater room where there were clips of women on a reel. Some of them were with men, others with women, and others were alone pleasuring themselves.

When I heard a loud moan, I turned to the naked woman lying on the floor with her hands and ankles bound separately through leather bindings. She wore a blindfold while the two males beside her held a candle. I watched them pour wax all over her skin, and she moaned loudly again. Her pale skin turned red in seconds, and their erections bounced in anticipation.

They were all getting off on it, and I couldn't help but feel the same.

It was as if I was watching it in slow motion, feeling the allure and magnetism tugging me forward. My panties got wet, and I squeezed my metal leash. Within seconds, both the men had their cocks in their hands, stroking up and down as my eyes widened. Jace pulled me out of the room when one of the men moved between her legs and the other to her mouth.

I saw two women exit the next room, which caught my eye. Jace noticed, walking us to it. He opened the door into a dim room where a few people were having sex in all positions. Some were straddling men, others were going at it with women, and some were even in groups, taking it in every hole. Through a fascinated regard, I watched as they sucked cock and ate pussy. My eyes couldn't focus on one thing for very long, and I swear my mouth hung open.

I had so many questions and not nearly enough answers.

Instead, my concentrated stare went back to the scenes unfolding in front of me as we walked through the rooms, one by one. Jace led me deeper into the rabbit hole, and I eagerly awaited what was next to come. Each room differed from the last. The only thing they had in common was the heady, palpable hedonism.

One of the back rooms caught my attention on our way through the maze. The crazy thing about it was that Jace sensed that too. In one quick, sudden movement, we were walking toward that door.

For some reason, at that exact moment, I was blatantly aware I had no control.

No power.

I couldn't have walked away, even if I wanted to.

And the terrifying thing about it…

Was that I didn't want to.

Right when we walked through that door, the music changed to "Moonlight Sonata" by Beethoven. It echoed off the walls. The door closed behind me, causing this second to feel that much more real for me.

A bed was in the middle of the open space, a sex swing was to the left, and a couch on the right. However, none of those things caught my attention like the couples against the wall.

They were watching.

Waiting.

For what?

My heart suddenly pounded profusely in my chest, and I swear everyone could hear it. Once Jace led me to the middle of the room, he grabbed me around the waist and unexpectedly held me tight against his hard cock that he didn't try to hide from me. I held in a gasp, not wanting them to know this was the first time I felt him in this way.

After all, I was supposed to be his wife.

Excitement began to course through me, making me wonder what was next. My panties were soaking wet, anxiously anticipating his next move.

Were we the entertainment? What the hell?

I surveyed the room, breathing in what could only be described as the smell of lust and pure abandonment.

Jace's hands slid their way up my thighs. His callused fingers caressed and kneaded at my already heightened flesh as Beethoven's melody continued to assault my senses, mimicking his hands on my body.

He rubbed his nose along the back and sides of my neck, rasping into my ear, "I don't even have to touch you to know you're soaking wet, Cove."

His touch felt like everything I ever wanted and didn't think I could have. At least not by him. It was so confusing that he was effortlessly marking me, and he was barely touching me yet.

He murmured in my ear, only loud enough for me to hear, "I need obedience, bunny, and I'll reward you for it."

Before I could react, his hand roamed toward my core. I couldn't resist the urge to moan when his fingers found the layer of silk right above my clit. The palm of his hand swayed back and forth on my pussy to the melody of the music for a moment. I could feel my moisture starting to seep through the thin fabric as his other hand slowly moved its way up my body.

Following his command, I leaned into his touch while his fingers ignited something unfamiliar deep within me. I didn't know where I wanted him to touch me the most.

My whole body was on fire.

He brazenly announced, "I don't know whether to use my hands or my mouth, Cove? Tell me, which do you want, bunny?"

Playing my role, I panted, "Whatever you want," as I swayed my ass against his rock-hard cock and silently pleaded for him to keep going.

How far was he going to take this?

Only then did I understand why these couples were in here in the first place. They were voyeurs, and I guess that made us exhibitionists. At first, Jace didn't touch me where I wanted him the most. Instead, he teased my pussy on top of my panties while his other hand slid down the front of my dress, freeing my breasts.

I should have stopped him.

I should have told him no.

I didn't.

I got lost in whatever was happening between us, pretending we were alone and not in a room full of strangers. My mask made it easy to hide behind, serving its purpose. I craved Jace's touch, longing to feel like I was his for what felt like forever.

I hated him, right?

The truth was, I wanted him to fuck me in this room, claim me in front of these people I'd never see again.

I wanted all that and more.

But mostly, I just desired him.

I bit my bottom lip as I watched a man get sucked off by a woman sitting on another man's face. Her head fell back, as mine did, and Jace took it as an open invitation to slide my panties over to rub my clit in a side-to-side motion.

No warning.

He wasn't soft.

Or gentle.

My eyes closed on their own as he continued to play me like his favorite toy.

"You close your eyes again, and I'll fucking stop," he warned. "I brought you here to watch, and I expect nothing less."

I whimpered when he bit me and opened my hooded gaze.

"Good girl," he whispered in my ear, sucking on my earlobe.

"Mmm…" I shamelessly moaned so close to coming from his sweet, skilled torture.

The asshole knew it too.

I leaned into his embrace, shamelessly begging, "Please, Jace. Please give me what I want," without him having to demand it.

"Is that what you want? To come on my hand in a room full of strangers?"

"Yes…"

"Good girl," he groaned.

I could feel his teeth nibbling my skin, making me feel both pleasure and pain. Grabbing the back of his head, I held him for support. I could hear the breathless pants all around me from the endless amounts of skin-on-skin contact, but I didn't care.

I was too far gone.

Jace grabbed my chin, turning my face to meet his lips.

Was he going to kiss me?

I didn't have to demand an answer because in one swift movement, his mouth was on mine. He wasn't just kissing me. This was all claim.

For them?

For me?

Or for him?

Before I could prepare for his attack, he slid his tongue into my mouth. I tasted him for the first time, and I knew right then and there I'd never be able to get enough of him. This was fucking with my mind.

He was fucking with my head.

I couldn't tell what was pretend or what was real. I wanted so desperately to believe he wanted this as much as I did. All this time, all these years, I thought I was over him.

Again, I was slapped in the face that my feelings for him were still there. Alive and thriving, becoming part of me.

Fuck...

This wasn't fair.

Why was he doing this to me?

It was for the mission, Cove. Nothing more, nothing less. Then why did it feel like my feelings were reciprocated?

The more he kissed me, touched me, made me feel like I was truly his, the further my infatuation for him grew.

Was it lust?

A crush?

Love?

I didn't know, and at that moment, I didn't care because I was in his arms, and that was good enough for me.

"I'm... I'm..."

"You going to come for me, bunny?"

"Yes..."

We stayed like that for what felt like an eternity, just enjoying the feel of one another. Until he wrapped his hand around my neck and squeezed lightly, locking me in place, holding me in front of him, not allowing me to move an inch.

He was in control.

Exactly how I wanted him to be.

I could feel my wetness dripping down his hand, and he didn't let up. If anything, he manipulated my clit with every strum of the instrumental song.

Faster.

Harder.

I ached to come.

"That's right..." he baited. "Just like that... give me what I want..."

I did.

I came, immediately seeing stars.

My villain.

My captor.

My hero.

Had now turned into…

My lover who made me come for the first time in my life.

CHAPTER 16
JACE

The silence was deafening on the drive back to the safe house. Her sweet scent still lingered on my fingers as I rubbed them in a back-and-forth motion over my mouth. Absentmindedly, I stared out the window, lost in my own thoughts.

We were sitting on opposite ends of the SUV, leaving shortly after our performance. Cove executed her role perfectly, and I'd be lying if I said I wasn't fazed by how amazing she felt in my arms. The way she willingly handed over her pleasure like it belonged to me wasn't something I would soon forget.

Her moans.

Her taste.

Whether I wanted it to be or not, it was now part of me.

The world I created for myself was now a fucking wreck. All because of the blond bunny sitting on the other end of the seat beside me. I could feel her emotions pumping new life into me in a way I hadn't experienced in a long time.

She was truly fucking with the control I prided myself on.

I didn't want to stop touching her and had to resist the urge to fuck her right then and there in a room full of strangers, which was very unlike me. I always took what I wanted. It was how I was made. End of story.

I couldn't take this bullshit silence anymore. It only triggered my reckless thoughts.

From the moment we stepped inside the safe house, I ordered, "Ask."

She didn't waver. "Why?"

"Why what, bunny?"

"Why did you take me there?"

"I told you. I had to make you get used to my touch."

"In a room full of strangers?"

"Consider it a crash course."

"Bullshit!"

"How many times do I have to tell you the less you know, the better?"

"It's too late for that!"

In one stride, I was in her face. "Does it look like I want to be yelled at?"

She shoved me, and I barely wavered.

"Fuck off!"

Not hesitating, I spewed, "I'd much rather fuck you."

She gasped, jerking back. Never expecting me to confess that.

"That's what you want to hear, right? How much I want to bury my face between your legs to make you come in my mouth? How about all the ways I can make you scream my goddamn name? With my fingers, my mouth, my cock... Cove, the things I can do to you would have you in love with me by the end of the night."

She swallowed hard. "Is this your plan? To humiliate me right now?"

"You haven't been paying attention, bunny. I'm not the man you think I am."

"Maybe you're not the man you think you are."

I narrowed my eyes at her. "What do you think is happening here? Just because I want to fuck you doesn't mean I'll ever love you."

Before the last word left my mouth, she slapped me across the face, and I'd be lying if I said I didn't expect her to.

She raised her hand to slap me again, but I caught it midair.

"I let you hit me *once*. It won't happen again."

She tried to yank her hand away, but it was useless to fight. I wasn't letting her go.

"Was this your plan? To make me crave you and the things you do to me?"

"No, that was just a bonus. I haven't done anything you didn't want or need."

"You fucking asshole!"

She went to knee me in the balls, but I used her momentum against her, spinning her around until her back was to my front. Not letting her move an inch, I held her in a lock hold against my chest.

"I hate you!" she roared. "Do you hear me? I. Hate. You!"

I allowed her to have her defiance. It was the least I could do after what I put her through tonight.

"I made you come, didn't I?"

She scoffed out in disgust. Her steep breaths came out in ragged pants while her chest rose and fell.

"Are you trying to make me hate you more than I already do?"

"Your manipulation doesn't work on me, Cove. If you hated me as much as you claim to, you wouldn't be giving me shit right now."

"That's not true!"

"What's not true? Huh? That if I slid my hand into your panties, they wouldn't be soaking wet for me?"

"You arrogant bastard!"

Through a clenched jaw, I sneered into her ear, "You're right. I'm an asshole. I'm a fucking bastard. I'm everything you need to stay far away from. Don't get this twisted, Cove. What happened between you and me tonight was all for show. My enemies were there, and they needed to know I was too."

"Then why am I pretending to be your wife?"

"It's the only way I can keep you safe, but don't get it fucking twisted. At the end of the day, I'm a man. You put a bone in front of a dog, it will want to eat it."

"So that's all I am to you? A pussy you want to eat?"

"No. You're also my little sister's best friend, and it's the only reason I'm keeping you safe. I refuse to let her lose another woman she loves."

I let her go, backing away from her.

When she turned, her eyes rimmed with tears. "What made you this way?"

I growled.

"Tell me what happened? I can help you," she urged.

In pity.

In pain.

"Don't fuck with me, Cove."

Her reply of, "Your mother would be so disappointed in you," had me fucking spinning.

It was only then she realized it wasn't a what question.

It was a who.

120

I shook my head, warning, "Don't..."

"I know what you do is dangerous. I know there's a reason you're like this." She stepped forward. "I know what it feels like to be alone, to feel like you have no one on your side. I'm here for you. Why won't you let me be?" she rasped, her voice giving out on her.

She reached for me.

I couldn't take this much longer.

I didn't want her sympathy.

Her concern.

Her love?

"Don't touch me, Cove. You need to stay away from me," I coaxed, moving her hands away from my body.

"Jace, please... please... just let me..." she pleaded in a tone of pure desperation and sorrow.

"Don't fucking touch me. I'm warning you. What will it take for you to realize I'm no good?!" I shouted, raking my hands through my hair.

She didn't listen, continuing her assault, trying to touch my face, my arms, and my chest. Her hands burned as if she was touching me with fire, dragging me further into hell, and coming right along with me. Her hands burned everywhere she placed them, everywhere she touched me, leaving behind deeper scars than the ones I already carried.

"Why won't you just let me in? I can help...we can help each other. Why do you insist on fighting with me?"

I roughly grabbed her wrists tighter than I intended to, holding her in place before I abruptly let her go. Without thinking twice about it, I turned and left, slamming the front door behind me.

I couldn't look at her anymore.

I couldn't hear her desperate pleas.

I couldn't feel her delicate touch trying to heal what was broken inside me.

I didn't go far. I had a job to do, and I intended to follow through. It didn't matter what she said or did; it wouldn't change the outcome of my life. I lived and breathed this world. It was the only way I could keep going through the hell I'd been through.

I left her there alone for one reason and one reason only. After this mission, I needed to figure out what it would take to rid her from my mind.

My life.

My future.

Before I killed her too.

CHAPTER 17
JACE

THEN: FIVE MONTHS AFTER TONY'S FUNERAL

Dear Hope,

When I received your first letter after Tony's service, I never expected to develop this relationship with you and actually start looking forward to your letters. You've brought this happiness and sunshine back into my life. You know that, don't you? And how much I care for you and your son. I think about you both more often than not. It almost feels like you were brought into my life for a reason I didn't know was missing.

I've never been the type of man who relied on a woman's affection, but with you, it's different. The guilt I carry because you were Tony's fiancée is another demon I can't eliminate. Not a day goes by when I don't think about him. Sometimes I even dream about him.

Except he wasn't the one who died in the line of fire.

I did.

Other times, I wished it would have been me, but then I think about the pain it would have caused my family. They don't deserve to lose another person they love. The first time was hard enough. I know it's selfish of me to pray for the souls I've taken, yet I can't stop myself from doing it.

I often think about where I'm going once I die because there's no chance it'll be heaven. It doesn't stop my desire to want to be free from the demons that live inside me.

I don't deserve it.

Which is why I don't pray for forgiveness. If anything, I pray for God to punish me. Maybe that's why I lost my mother? I can't stop my mind from going there.

Was her death my punishment?

Was Tony's?

I've never shared these thoughts with anyone, but with you, it's different. It's easy. Almost like we were meant to find each other. You've been such a breath of fresh air in my life, and I couldn't imagine you not being in it.

You're part of me now.

You both are.

I can't wait to see you next month. Hold you. Feel you. It's what gets me through most nights. I know I don't deserve you either, but I can't stop myself. I see a future with you and your son, and that scares me more than anything. I've never felt this way about anyone before, Hope. I promised Tony I'd take care of you both, but you're so much more than a promise to me.

The nights when I'm on missions are some of the loneliest times of my life. I have nothing to distract myself with. It doesn't matter how exhausted

I am or how much I push my body physically and mentally, sleep never comes easily for me.

My memories were always there.

The bad ones always outweighed the good.

There were times when I couldn't shake them off as much as I tried to. They wouldn't let me go, strangling me until I couldn't fucking breathe. Like a noose around my neck, sucking the life right out of me.

Sometimes I welcomed that feeling.

At least then I knew I was still fucking alive.

Ever since you came into my life, I find myself looking forward to a future with you both. No amount of training could have prepared me for the things I'd seen and done. My kill or be killed mentality has left me alone with only my thoughts and memories.

Because the truth is…

I'm falling in love with you and your baby, and I know you feel the same.

With all my love,

Sincerely, Jace

CHAPTER 18
COVE
NOW: TWO DAYS LATER

To say I was annoyed with the past forty-eight hours would be an understatement. We'd been playing newlyweds all over the island. From one end to the other, we pretended to be in love. To an outsider looking in, we were happily married, but as soon as we were behind closed doors, Jace barely talked to me.

Despite us sleeping in the same bed, he hadn't touched me since the night of the sex party. Not that I didn't want him to.

One thing was for sure, Jace didn't sleep much. The man seemed to survive on two, maybe three hours a night. When he finally would lay down, his sleep was restless. He'd toss and turn most of the time, and I desperately wanted to know what he was dreaming about. I yearned to know what haunted him even in his slumber.

It didn't matter how much I wanted him to open up to me, I knew he wouldn't. He refused to let me in, and I began to wonder if he ever would or if this was forever our dynamic.

What would happen after we went back home? Were we just supposed to pretend this never happened? Had my parents noticed I was gone? Were they searching for me? Was anyone?

Haven was still overseas with her boyfriend, and we weren't talking much before this happened. She was enjoying her time with him, and I didn't want to interrupt them. I understood they needed this time to reconnect with each other, and I was happy they had that opportunity.

I didn't have my cell phone, so I didn't know if my parents were trying to reach me. Although, that was pretty far-fetched. They had always lived their own life. I wouldn't be surprised if they even noticed I was gone, which made me sad.

I truly didn't have anyone who loved or cared about me other than my best friend. If she knew I'd technically been kidnapped, she'd be searching hell and high water for me. That much I was sure of.

Jace's family certainly didn't know about his double life. I figured no one knew the man behind the uniform, and that made me so unbelievably sad for him. I knew what it felt like to be alone. If I didn't have Haven or his family, I'd be very lonely on the daily, but it didn't matter how much I had Haven's friendship, I longed for my parents.

Jace came up behind me, wrapping his arms around my waist. "Have I told you how beautiful you look in that dress?"

I smiled, leaning against the railing at the Coco Beach Club.

"You haven't, but I'm sure you could make it up to me somehow."

Everywhere we went, it felt as if all eyes were on us. I couldn't tell if it was his enemies, or we just looked good together and brought attention to ourselves. It was difficult to tell the difference.

Jace played his part of the loving, affectionate husband like he was born for the role. He was attentive, doting, and always had his hands on me in one way or another. Even when we were eating, his hand would be on my lap or his arm around my chair.

This French island had thirty-seven beaches, and we'd probably visited half of them, playing the part of being madly in love the entire time. We'd gone everywhere—the casino where he won a couple of thousand dollars playing poker, the day pool parties where Jace really wouldn't keep his hands off me since I was wearing a bikini, the nightclubs, and eating breakfast, lunch, and dinner at the most breathtaking restaurants.

There wasn't anything that Jace Beckham wasn't good at. The man was as gifted as he was charming. The way women stumbled over their words when they were talking to him or how they couldn't take their eyes off him when he walked into any room.

Again, it was beyond fucking annoying.

Jace turned me in his arms, and under the full moon and stars, he expressed, "I can't take my eyes off you," before he kissed me.

The good and the bad.

His heaven and hell.

Pleasure and pain.

It all blended together now.

The villain was no longer present, he'd been replaced by my hero, simply adding to all my conflicting emotions wreaking havoc all around me. I'd awakened the sleeping beast, and he'd finally come out to play.

In a sick and twisted way, I wanted this.

His control.

His hands.

His body.

I craved every last part of him.

Jace kissed my lips with so much urgency that I could have come from that alone. When his tongue touched mine, I inadvertently moaned.

This was happening.

Jace had become my make-believe happily ever after, and I was helpless not to fall for his deviousness.

By the time we left the restaurant that turned into a nightclub after ten, it was almost midnight. Jace parked the Audi sports car he rented for the day in the lot farther away from the establishment because we couldn't find parking. The lot where he did find a spot was also packed, but now it was completely empty.

Leading me to the car, Jace opened the passenger door, and I stepped inside. Once he was in the driver's seat, it all happened in a flash. Although it still felt like it played out in slow motion for what felt like the hundredth time in just a couple of days.

Jace revved the engine hard and fast as bullets started lacing the back of our car, shattering the rear windshield. In seconds, my adrenaline pumped wildly through my veins as it purred to life. I felt every fight-or-flight response known to man in a short amount of time.

"Oh my God!" I screamed.

Jace roared, "Put your head down and hang on!"

Quickly shifting the gear into second, he tore through the streets before shifting into third as bullets continued to ring out behind us.

Fifty miles per hour.

Sixty.

Seventy-five.

He gunned it down the road, kicking up dirt in our wake. I watched in astonishment as he downshifted to first, fishtailing out onto another open road where he nearly caused a collision with a dumpster truck. The only sounds that could be heard were the squealing tires of everyone's vehicles and shots being fired, shattering more windows and metal on our car.

Jace returned fire, blowing out the tires of one of the cars chasing us.

"Fuck, Cove! I'm out of ammo! There's more under the seat! I need you to get it for me!"

More bullets bounced off our sportscar while I reached for the bag in the back seat, pulling out two guns. The rush surging through my veins controlled my actions as my hands shook uncontrollably, but I acted on pure impulse and quickly grabbed the wheel.

"Cove, what are you—"

"You need to focus! I can do this!"

He reluctantly nodded before several shots were fired through the air.

More bullets pinged off the metal.

More glass shattered all around us.

More.

More.

More.

Driving as best as I could, I moved on pure fear. Staying low, Jace shot out the window while ducking from the breaking glass.

"How many cars?" I shouted through the chaos, hearing one of the cars spinning out of control.

"Three!"

"Are we going to—"

"Fuck this shit!"

I watched in horror as Jace leaned out the window, shooting in all directions to take out their windshields.

"Now we're down to two," he announced, sitting back in the driver's seat.

While Jace reloaded, I weaved in and out of the streets. Thank God there weren't any cars out other than us. I would have felt horrible if someone else was hurt.

How did Jace do this? Is this why he was so unbelievably broken?

My gaze zeroed in when I saw the scene unfolding in front of us. All the air in my lungs halted as my intense glare focused on the road signs indicating it was closed.

"Jace..."

Before I could finish my warning, he downshifted at the last second, jerking the wheel out of my hands to make a sharp right turn. Our car slid, missing the road signs, but the car behind us wasn't so lucky and crashed into it.

The next string of bullets rang out, missing my head by mere inches. However, Jace's shoulder was hit. He didn't even blink; he was unfazed by the bullet that grazed his skin.

He over-revved the engine, shifting into fourth gear. Our endorphins skyrocketed, bringing me to my fucking breaking point. It took over every inch of my body.

"Jace, you've been hit!" I exclaimed, thinking he didn't feel it.

It wasn't until he yanked up the emergency brake and slammed his foot on the brake that I understood where his mind was at. He simultaneously jerked the wheel to the left, causing my petite frame to be tossed toward the passenger side door as our car spun out in a one-eighty.

This was beyond surreal. It was like a high-speed chase you'd see in a special ops movie where the car parallels perfectly to the enemy's window, exactly how he knew it would. The enemy's eyes widened when he realized Jace had his gun pointed at the center of his face. Directly between his eyes.

In less than a second, Jace released his fury in a way I'd never seen before in real life. Shot after shot erupted from his gun, sending the enemy into convulsive shaking from the bullets lacing his entire body.

"Jace! He's dead! Stop!"

He shot him a few more times, being ruthless and unforgiving.

"He almost killed you, Cove! Fuck him!"

He wouldn't stop.

It was like he went into complete soldier mode. Again, I'd never seen anything like it before in reality. This wasn't a movie, and Jace wasn't an actor. He was the man I had a crush on since I was eight years old.

I knew he wouldn't stop—he was too far gone. Reaching over, I acted on instinct, placing my hand on his forearm to bring him back to me.

Only then did his gaze shift to my hold before he locked eyes with me. However, it wasn't Jace's stare I was looking at. It was someone else's entirely.

I didn't know this man.

He wasn't familiar.

I didn't even recognize him.

At that moment, he was a complete and utter stranger.

So much passed through his tormented expression, and he didn't try to hide it from me like he usually did. In a matter of seconds, Jace showed me how truly broken he was. Jace may have been sitting there with me, but his mind was elsewhere.

"Hey…" I coaxed, caressing the side of his face. "I'm okay, Jace… I'm okay."

The second I touched his skin, he shook away the turmoil.

Backing away from my touch, he threw the shifter into first and drove us the hell out of there.

My chest heaved, trying to catch my breath as I pointed out the obvious. "You've been hit."

"The bullet just grazed me. I'm fine."

Once again annoyed, I stated, "You can't keep doing this. You can't keep pushing me away. I may be young, but I'm not that naive. I see the shadows you're desperately trying to hide from me, but I still don't understand why. You can trust me. I don't know how I can prove that any more than I already have."

He didn't say a word, and the ride back to the safe house was quiet, but the silence did very little for my pissed-off state of mind.

Maybe it was the near-death experience.

Or the fear.

The hopelessness.

Or maybe it was my endless thought process of what was yet to come.

I had no control, no say, nothing. As soon as we walked through the front door into the dining room, my patience desperately snapped.

Unable to hold back, I laid into him, "How much longer do you expect to do this to me?"

I was fully aware this wouldn't end well, and for the first time...

I didn't give a flying fuck if it did.

CHAPTER 19
COVE

"**B**unny…"

"Don't bunny me, G.I. Joe! I'm sick and tired of your mind games! You're hot, you're cold, and all your multiple personalities are giving me whiplash!"

"Not. Right. Now."

He abruptly turned, and I didn't waver. Grabbing the glass vase off the table, I chucked it at his head. Being the soldier he was, he ducked, and it crashed into the wall behind him.

He snapped around, growling, "You want to throw things at me like a fucking child?! You need to learn how to control your tantrums, bunny! I'm sick and tired of your constant stream of nothing but bullshit!"

My eyes widened, cocking my head to the side. "Oh, asshole! I'll show you a tantrum!" I reached for whatever was in sight, hurling it in his direction with all my strength. "You selfish son of a bitch!"

His hands fisted at his sides.

"Enough!" he ordered from deep within his chest.

Our chests heaved in sync with one another. Both of our heated emotions were running wild.

I could feel his hate.

But I could also feel his protection and concern over me. The barricade surrounding his heart was a ticking time bomb, counting down the minutes until it exploded.

It was loud.

Disastrous.

Chaotic.

It would take down everything around him with it, like a tornado spinning around in circles. It elicited feelings from within me that I never thought were possible, emotions no one should ever have to experience.

I felt every loss of breath.

All his hurt.

His distress.

His anguish for me.

Which was why he was pissed off to begin with. I was almost hurt on his watch. If the bullets had been a couple of inches to the left, I would have died instantly from them shooting me in the head.

Nothing of that sort happened, yet he couldn't forgive himself for it. I tried to keep my feelings in check, but they cluttered my mind, willing me to keep going, to push through.

I couldn't give up on him.

I refused.

His mom wouldn't want me to.

I needed a reaction out of him, so I said the only thing that came to mind, shouting, "I hate you!"

He was over to me before I even saw it coming as I repeated, "I hate y—"

With one hand over my throat, he slammed my back against the wall behind me, growling against my lips, "You wish you fucking hated me."

Then he crashed his mouth onto mine.

Jace

My hands dug into her hair, and hers clawed at my chest.

It was powerful.

It was deprived.

It was everything.

She met each push and pull I delivered, gripping the sides of my face as my tongue devoured her perfect pouty lips.

Her soft tongue.

Her scent.

With her fucking body pressed up against mine, I groaned, getting lost in the feel of her. Nothing compared to this.

To her.

Cove Noel was my kryptonite, and I knew that more than anything.

She forcefully gripped the front of my shirt, yanking me closer like we weren't already close enough. Trying to mold us into one person, she kissed me as if her life depended on it. Moaning into my mouth, she stirred my cock to twitch in my slacks.

"Fuck... Cove..." I grabbed her hair by the nape of her neck, yanking it back. Putting some much-needed distance between us, I rasped, "What are you doing to me, bunny?"

She panted, frantically trying to gather her bearings from my tight hold. Both our bodies shook with undeniable desire. Every part of my resolve hammered all around us.

I could hear it in my ears.

I could feel it deep in my bones.

Breaching the walls I securely had in place when it came to her. Every part of my nervous system was breaking, shutting down, making it hard to see, let alone stand.

I didn't know if it was the car chase.

The arguing between us.

Or the fact she almost died that had me feeling fucking alive for the first time in what felt like decades.

It was thrilling.

It was captivating.

I knew it was from *her*.

It had everything to do with her.

She weakly thrashed around some more, ignoring the pain in her head and the ache in her heart I was inflicting. I held her tighter against my chest, both of us gasping for air.

She infuriatingly screamed, and I was unaware if it was from what I said or from knowing it was the truth. Or possibly from knowing she wasn't going anywhere unless I allowed her to. Closing her eyes, she tried to govern her breathing and her thoughts.

I loosened my grip, slowly brushing my lips against hers. I saw memories passing through her eyes, attacking her mind rapidly.

"Tell me…"

"No."

"Bunny..."

"No."

She turned her face away from mine, but I gripped her chin, forcing her to peer back up at me. I wanted a moment to caress her.

To gaze at her.

To embrace her.

To fucking feel her.

We stared at each other for what felt like hours, both of us lost in our own thoughts.

In our own demons.

I rubbed her bottom lip with my thumb, reveling in the feel of her velvety skin.

"I fucking hate you," she panted before crashing her mouth onto mine.

I snarled, parting her lips with my tongue as my hands slid to the seam of her tight dress, hiking it up to her hips as I lifted her to straddle my waist. She winced from the loss of my touch when I set her on the edge of the table, but it wasn't missing for very long.

Unable to fight it any longer, I gave in to the temptation that was this woman without even trying.

Without thinking twice about it, I dropped to my knees between her legs, needing to taste her.

Wanting to eat her.

Craving to fuck her pussy with my tongue.

There was no way in hell I wasn't going to devour her with my mouth. I was a greedy bastard. I inhaled her intoxicating scent, softly kissing around her folds. She gasped when she felt my tongue on her heat as I slid it into the opening of her sweet, salty cunt.

She was pink.

She was wet.

She was fucking perfect.

And tasted like everything I ever wanted.

"Oh God," she moaned as I placed her thighs onto my shoulders. Her hands instantly fisted in my hair, tugging it to the point of pain.

I knew her body better than she did. These past few days, I couldn't keep my hands off her. Like a man on a mission, I took what I hunted.

Looking up at her, I kneaded her tits. Sucking her clit into my mouth, I moved my head in a side-to-side and back-and-forth motion.

"Ah!" she yelled out, trying to catch her bearings.

Her chest heaved with every precise manipulation of my lips and tongue. My mouth literally ate her alive. Watching as I gave her what she really wanted since the moment she woke up in this safe house.

I licked her one last time and then stopped, baiting, "Tell me you want it, bunny. Fucking beg me for it."

"Please," she moaned.

I growled and returned to lapping at her pussy, making her go crazy with passion. I knew these were feelings only I could ever elicit from her.

Within seconds, I was making her come hard and fast. She shook the entire time as I let her ride out her orgasm against my mouth before I released her with a pop. I didn't bother wiping her come from my face, attacking her mouth instead.

With my hand at the back of her neck to keep her locked close to me, it was exactly where I wanted her to be. She tasted every last bit of herself, loving how much of a dirty bastard I was.

Being the asshole that I was, I taunted, "Your pussy doesn't hate. Does that taste like hate to you?" I suddenly grabbed a fistful of her hair.

She yelped at the unexpected intrusion on her scalp.

"Isn't that right?"

Forcefully, I yanked her head back farther, taking ahold of her face and squeezing her jaw. Needing her to see she wasn't going to win this power struggle between us.

This was far from over.

In fact, it was only the beginning.

I let her go at a moment's notice because if I didn't…

I'd claim her virginity and fuck her raw and senseless.

To hell with the goddamn consequences.

CHAPTER 20
COVE

I felt his presence before I actually saw him. His masculine scent immediately assaulted my senses. He was lying shirtless on his back with one defined, toned arm underneath his pillow behind his head.

I was under the sheets while he lay on top of them on the bed beside me. The position he was passed out in accentuated his chiseled abs and bare chest, leaving very little to the imagination.

I couldn't help but look down at his gym shorts. His bulging cock also lay there proudly between his legs. He wasn't even hard, and it still appeared massive through the thin cotton fabric.

I rolled onto the side of my body, staring at him for a few minutes to just admire him, taking in every last inch of this man's muscular physique. He truly was a work of art. Being this handsome should be a sin. Even in his sleep, he exuded dominance.

I couldn't take my mesmerized gaze off him.

After he finished going down on me, I probably lay on that table for who knows how long. Jace of course left through the front door once he was done, slamming it behind him like he was pissed at what happened between us in the first place.

On the other hand, I didn't know what to say or feel. All I knew were that my emotions were running wild when it came to him, and what he did to me earlier that night simply intensified it tenfold. It was my first time having someone do that to me, and all I wanted was to call Haven and tell her, but I couldn't, and that was probably one of the hardest pills to swallow.

This was the first time I couldn't tell my best friend about what was occurring in my life, and it plagued me. I wanted to ask for her advice. She was the best person to talk to about anything and not having that support was just as hard as whatever was happening between us. I was young and naive, and he was a man after all. However, age was just a number, despite us being twenty years apart.

I took a shower before coming to bed, leaning my forehead against the ceramic tile to let the scalding hot water run down my back, welcoming the burn. My body physically ached for some rest, some sleep, something, anything that would make my mind stop running wild like a hamster spinning on a fucking wheel.

I stayed in there until the water ran cold, and then got out. Throwing on one of Jace's shirts that still smelled like him, I brushed my teeth, gargled some mouthwash, and then lay down on the bed.

My plan was to wait up for him, but in the end, sleep quickly won out. I had no clue when he came to bed, but all that mattered was he was there with me now. My eyes shifted to the clock on the nightstand and saw it read 4:00 a.m.

I silently wished he would take me in his arms and tell me what he was feeling, though I knew he never would. Tonight was a whirlwind of emotions. I was scared and nervous of what was to come and not knowing what it could be simply made it much harder than it probably needed to be. I couldn't prepare myself for anything. I was just along for the ride and hanging on for dear life.

Hoping.

Praying.

That maybe he felt the same way I did.

All of this was just making me feel closer to him, I wanted to be with him now more than ever. It was as if his dark side was luring me in, the pull he had on me was palpable, and I could no longer resist my feelings for him. The longer I lay there, the further I realized this was where I belonged.

With him.

In his bed, falling asleep next to him every night, and waking up to him every morning. I didn't want to be alone anymore, and a huge part of me knew he didn't either.

My fingers glided along the sheets, feeling the soft fabric under my touch. Careful not to wake him, I scooted my body up to lay next to his as I finally felt at peace with his presence beside me.

His breathing was calming, calling out for me to touch him.

It all happened so fast, exactly the way everything had since the night he killed Deacon. I decided it was time for me to return the favor, surprising him with a blow job to see what kind of effect I had on him.

One minute, my hand was in the air, reaching to pull away the waistband of his gym shorts, but the instant I softly touched the edge, he roughly flipped me onto my back with his hand over my neck.

I gasped loudly, caught off guard and taken by surprise.

However, that wasn't the worst part.

This was minimal compared to the gun suddenly pressed to the side of my head, right on my temple. His body hovered on top of mine, his heavy weight laying directly on top of my small frame. His face was inches away from mine as he opened his dark, dilated eyes that were vacant of any life.

My chest heaved.

My breath quickened.

My heart hammered out of my chest.

Jace didn't remove his hold or his gun as he glared at me with something I couldn't place in his murderous stare. Once again, it was like he was there with me, but at the same time, he was somewhere else entirely.

It didn't stop the emotions from pouring out of me and onto the sheets behind my body. They tethered between us. I felt as if I saw his past and present colliding with a force brought on by me. Nothing of what I thought would happen did.

Not one fucking thing.

The truth lay on top of the chaos he created in my mind. The pieces of his puzzle held so many unanswered questions which still loomed in the distance between us.

My heart was breaking for him.

Except this time, I felt like I couldn't take it anymore. His demons were pulling me under, dragging me further into the ground and the hell he created for himself. His truths were burning me alive and at the stake.

I was trying to save him, and for the first time, I understood that maybe he was trying not to destroy me in the process. Through the soft lighting of the moon, darkness fell over us through the curtains that were slightly opened.

In a moment of weakness, I surrendered to the power he had over me, and I wasn't talking about his current hold on my throat.

I was the first to break the connection between us, fixing my stare to the gun at my temple.

"Do you want me to fucking kill you, Cove?"

My trembling hands fisted the sheets. There was so much I wanted to say, and I kept opening my mouth, only to close it several times, not knowing what would come out.

I didn't know where to start or where we stood.

My lips were swollen from sleep while my face was flushed, sweat glistened down the sides of my temples. I feared he was going to hurt me more than he already had at this point.

Never breaking our intense stare, he slowly started sliding his gun down the side of my face, my neck, and stopping on my chest, over my heart.

My breathing hitched.

"What did you think would happen if you woke me up like that?"

My mouth shut, swallowing hard as I licked my lips.

"After everything you've learned about me these past few days. Do you think I'm the man you take by surprise? No matter where I am, I sleep with a gun in my grasp under my pillow. I'm trained to kill, Cove. So I'll ask you again…" He didn't waver, speaking with conviction…

"Do you want me to hurt you?"

CHAPTER 21
COVE

Nothing about his confession surprised me. Nothing about the feelings I had for him did either. I was finally in his arms, feeling his skin against mine, loving the way he was looking at me. My mind had been spiraling out of control all day, and this only added to the tsunami of emotions coursing through me.

I wanted him more than reason.

More than what was right or what was wrong.

I wanted him more than anything.

There was no turning back, only going forward. Even if it meant he'd continue dragging me down into his inferno where he lived and breathed.

"Tell me, bunny. Do you like being at my fucking mercy?"

Before I could retort, he grinded his now hard cock against my pussy. Hitting my clit, and driving me crazy. I shuddered beneath him, moaning with each thrust of his hips. My wetness seeped through the silk of my panties.

I whimpered when he lifted his body off mine, taking his shirt with him. He lifted it to expose my breasts and stomach before continuing to glide his gun down my torso, leaving a trail of desire in his wake.

Now why this was turning me on was a whole other story… Probably one I'd eventually tell a therapist one day because this shit wasn't normal.

Who got off on a gun that could literally kill you?

I should have been terrified, wanting to run away from him and never look back, but I wasn't.

I wanted this.

Calling me out, he confidently teased, "You like this, Cove?"

I boldly nodded.

When he skimmed the gun along the edge of the top of my panties, my thighs clenched.

"Your body aches for me, begging me to touch it."

I moaned in response as he slid my panties to the side with his gun, causing me to quiver when the cold air came in contact with my bare folds.

Was he really going to do this?

In an attempt at enticing him to keep going, I smirked. With the barrel of the side of his gun, he started rubbing my clit up and down with the cool metal.

"You trust me this much?"

Was this another test?

Another game?

Burning his match, I lit it with one word. "Yes."

Our eyes stayed connected, and for a moment, I saw a familiar possessive regard pass through his expression, knowing I meant it. My lust-filled gaze showed him everything he needed to see and know. They spoke volumes for me.

He cocked his head to the side, sliding it faster and harder against my clit. "You're so fucking wet."

He didn't have to be told twice. He knew what he was doing.

Faster and faster.

"Fuck," he groaned, craving the same thing I did.

"Oh God…" I was on the brink of coming apart.

My body trembled.

My legs shook.

My back arched off the bed.

I screamed out, "Jace!" Climaxing so fucking hard my eyes rolled to the back of my head before I melted into the mattress, so heavy, so satiated, so consumed with his control over me.

My eyes were serene.

My body lax.

My cheeks flushed.

I swear I could have come again just from watching him lift the gun and lick my juices down the side of the barrel.

In a sharp, hulkingly tone, he declared, "You're my favorite thing to fucking eat."

With that, he tossed the gun onto the nightstand. I reached for his gym shorts again, pulling the elastic back to grab his dick, but he stopped me from returning the favor.

"No, bunny," he ordered in a calm voice, peering deep into my eyes.

My eyebrows narrowed, confused with his reaction. "But I—"

"I know what you want, but it's not happening."

"Why? It's not fair that I'm not giving you anything in return."

"Trust me, Cove. You're giving me more than enough."

Unable to resist, I questioned, "Have you ever done that before?"

"Which part?"

"You know what I mean…"

He devilishly grinned. "I still want to hear you say it."

"If I knew how to say it, then I would have already."

He scoffed out a chuckle.

"Your gun on my"—I wiggled my eyebrows—"you know…"

"Your sweet little pussy?"

I tried to pull the blanket over my face from embarrassment. "Jace…"

"I just made you come from my gun on your cunt, and now you're being shy?"

I giggled. "You obviously wanted me to trust you. Did I pass another one of your stimulating little tests?"

"There's nothing little about me, bunny."

"Jace, I was kidd—"

"It's late. You need to get some sleep."

He was about to get off the bed, but it was my turn to stop him.

I grabbed his arm, blurting, "Please don't leave. I don't like feeling used."

"Is that what you think I'm doing?"

I shrugged.

From the expression on his face, I thought he was going to leave me again, but instead, he lay down and brought me with him, placing me on his chest. Surprised he gave in to my demands, I curled into his embrace, nuzzling his torso with an arm draped across.

"Stop thinking, bunny. Just go to sleep."

"Are you?"

"I don't need much sleep."

"I've noticed that about you," I persistently stated, dying for him to let me in a bit. "Is there a reason for that?"

"You don't have a subtle bone in your body, do you?"

"I mean... I barely know anything about you, and I've already let you into my panties, so... how about you throw me a bone here?"

He didn't reply for what seemed like forever until finally, he shared, "It's a combination of things. Some of it's military, and others it's—"

"PTSD?"

"Something like that."

"Have you ever talked to someone about it?"

"What do you think?"

"Yeah..." I hesitated for second. "Well... you can always talk to me."

Again, nothing but silence like he was debating if he was going to share more until he added, "I'm not much for talking." He began rubbing my back.

"Believe it or not, I'm the same way. Haven has to pry it out of me most of the time."

"Haven has that effect on people. She's like our mom."

I smiled, drawing lazy circles around his chest. "The very first memory I have of your mom was Halloween. I didn't have a costume. My parents always forgot stuff like that. I remember our driver dropped me off at your house because your mom was going to take us trick-or-treating. Haven ran out to greet me, and she was wearing a full-on princess gown costume with the biggest crown. As soon as your mom saw me with no costume on, she just knew. An hour later, she came into Haven's bedroom with my very own princess gown costume. It was even my favorite color."

"Teal."

I jerked back, peering up at him. "How do you know that?"

"Haven's room was next to mine, remember?"

"Right... I don't know how your mom bought it on such short notice, but—"

150

"She made it."

I arched an eyebrow, waiting on pins and needles for him to elaborate.

"I had to run out and get her more fabric."

"You're lying."

"Of all the things to lie to you about, you think I'd start there?"

My afflicting emotions stirred all around us.

Consuming me.

Him.

Us?

"I had no idea you did that for me. That meant a lot to me, Jace. Thank you."

As I lay there with his arms wrapped around me, I got lost in what he had just openly confessed, and it was at that moment I realized I was truly screwed because I was beginning to fall in love with my best friend's brother.

Who was also hired to kill me.

CHAPTER 22
JACE

THEN: ONE MONTH LATER

"Where are we going?" Hope asked, sitting beside me on the plane.

Yesterday morning, I flew into her state to see her for the third time since Tony died. My second visit was short; I was only there for a couple of days. During dinner last night, I casually mentioned we were taking a much-needed vacation. I couldn't remember the last time I'd taken one.

She pretty much jumped in my lap the minute I told her I was taking her away. She kissed all over my face, expressing so much sincere joy. Last month, she moved into the new apartment I was paying for her. There were too many memories of Tony and the life they'd never have where she was living before.

The place was a three-bedroom, three-bath that overlooked the city of Miami. I was making more than enough money to help her and her unborn son financially. I promised Tony I'd take care of them, and I intended to follow through.

In the past six months, we'd probably written hundreds of letters to each other. Sometimes it felt like I knew her better than I knew myself.

"You asking me every five minutes isn't going to change my answer."

"I thought we were on vacation, Jace." She nodded to my laptop. "Why are you still working?"

"I have to take care of some things before we land."

"Which is where?"

I glanced at her. "Nice try."

I smiled, feeling as if I was a different man when I was with her. My past was behind me, and all I had to do was focus on the future. We bonded over the pain of losing Tony. It was what brought us together to begin with.

It seemed like my demons were asleep when I was around her. They subsided, letting me breathe for a minute. Something about our relationship was missing in my life, and I couldn't have been more grateful to have her.

Hope was so fucking pretty, growing this beautiful boy inside her body. She was adorable, pregnant stomach and all, with her overalls on. Pregnancy agreed with her.

Despite having these intense feelings for each other, we hadn't had sex. We just couldn't cross that bridge. I was content to have her sleeping in my arms. It was enough for me.

She let me finish my work for the rest of the flight while I rubbed her stomach. Once we landed, I grabbed her hand and led her off the plane and down the stairs to pick up our luggage. A chauffeured SUV waited for us at the airport to drive us to the private house I rented for the week.

"Ahhh! We're in St. Martin!" she exclaimed the second she realized where we were on the ride to the property.

We turned down a secluded path with palm trees on either side and drove for about ten minutes. Beautiful tropical trees mixed with lush greenery took up the sides of the road. You couldn't see anything behind the landscaped walls as we sped closer to our destination.

We'd have secluded privacy. It was what I wanted. Our own little oasis away from everything and everyone. The driveway to the house was about a hundred yards, leading to a roundabout where the driver parked. I grabbed her hand before opening the door to step out onto the limestone pavers that led all around the private estate.

I could smell the salty breeze coming off the water as I led us up to the house while the driver brought in our luggage behind us. I opened the courtyard doors and typed in the code to reveal grand, angled stairs that led us inside a coastal-themed home.

Her jaw dropped, turning in a full circle to take in her surroundings. The sunlight streamed through every window in the wide-open space, illuminating the space. I paid the driver and thanked him, closing the door behind him after he left.

"I can't believe you did this! This place is gorgeous, Jace."

I smiled, kissing her lips. "I'd do anything for you."

I followed her out to the balcony, setting my elbows on the railing as I inhaled a deep breath, looking out at the sun reflecting off the water. It was truly breathtaking, everything was.

Including her.

I felt Hope come up behind me, wanting to embrace the broken man in front of her with her son between us.

"I've never seen such an incredible property in all my life. I can't wait to experience this island with you."

For the next few days, we did exactly that. We spent our days relaxing, talking, and swimming in the pool or sightseeing around the island. Everywhere she wanted to go, I made sure I drove her to it. Our nights were spent lying together out on the lounger in the patio, staring out at the bright stars.

Hope was wrapped in my arms. We gazed up at the night sky, watching the full moon over the horizon and above the water. Sometimes we would talk, and other times we wouldn't. There was no need for words since our connection spoke for itself.

She passed out in my bed every night, and I'd try to find sleep that never came for me. I'd watch her rest. The way her chest would rise and fall with each breath, or how her pouty lips would part, and her hair cascaded all around her face.

She was so content.

Happy.

Fucking picturesque.

It brought me great joy knowing I was the cause.

Late into the night, I would slip out of the room, leaving her alone. I'd go out on the balcony and watch my life play out in front of me, trying to find peace in this heaven. Silently hoping that Tony's soul was resting and he was pleased with me taking care of his girl and not rolling over in his grave because of it.

I couldn't bring myself to be intimate with her. The guilt was too heavy.

Every morning the sun would come up, and Hope would wake, knowing where I was. She'd lay with me, setting her head on my lap as I ran my fingers through her soft brown hair.

She was only an angel in the house with me.

Tonight, we were once again lying out on the lounger, both of us lost in our own thoughts while her head rested on my chest as I caressed the side of her arm.

"Do you want your own children?" she asked out of nowhere.

"Where did that come from?"

"I'm just wondering."

"You know I'm going to take care of both of you, Hope."

"I know... but you haven't touched me this entire time, and we've already been here four days."

"I'm touching you right now."

"You know what I mean. It's Tony, isn't it?"

I didn't reply. I didn't have to.

"He loved you, you know? He thought of you as a brother."

"Which only makes what's happening between us that much harder."

"I know."

"I'm sorry, I can't give you what you want."

"It's hard for me too, Jace, but if it wasn't for you, I don't know where I'd be after losing him." Her eyes rimmed with tears. "I miss him every day. Sometimes I wake up and I think he's still alive, and then I remember I've lost him."

I nodded, understanding how she was feeling. I felt it too.

"You were his world, Hope."

"Where does that leave us?"

I didn't waver in admitting, "We're just living in the moment. It's all I have left to give you."

She nodded in understanding.

I couldn't help but wonder if she'd still feel the same way about me if she knew...

I killed her fiancé.

CHAPTER 23
JACE
NOW: THE NEXT MORNING

S he woke up to the smell of bacon and coffee, walking into the kitchen as I cooked breakfast.

"What are you doing?" she asked.

I turned to find her messy bedhead.

Her pouty pink lips swollen from sleep.

She was still wearing my shirt, making my cock twitch at the sight of her.

There was no taking my eyes off her beauty. She was fucking stunning, standing there with her bright blond hair that shined in the rays of the sunlight coming in through the bay window. Her soft, creamy skin was flawless.

She looked like a dream.

My dream or more like my worst nightmare.

She stood there, lost in her own little world. A world I desperately wanted to be a part of but knew that I never could.

I gazed at her gorgeous face, willing myself to stay where I was and not take her in my arms again. She slept on my chest the entire night as I rubbed her back and hair.

"Happy birthday, Cove."

She gasped with immediate tears brimming in her blue eyes. "How did you know—"

"Bunny, I've known you since you were four."

"But with your career, you were barely around."

"And when I was, you lived at our house."

"Right…" She winced. "I remember that bothered you."

I gave her a questioning expression. "What are you talking about?"

"Never mind." She shook her head. "Does that mean you made me breakfast for my birthday?"

Not backing down, I warned, "I don't like repeating myself. I asked you a question, and I expect an answer."

"I don't want to ruin this moment between us by bringing up the past."

"Stop pussyfooting around, Cove. I'm done waiting."

"Fine. You're so bossy." She sighed. "Your mom's funeral, remember? I followed you out to the stream behind your house."

I narrowed my eyes at her, taking in what she was saying.

"I shouldn't have invaded your personal space. I was just a stupid little girl trying to make you feel better."

I opened my mouth to reply, but I was interrupted by my cell phone ringing in the pocket of my jeans.

I answered, "Yeah?"

A familiar voice asked, "How's it going?"

Holding my hand over the mouthpiece of my phone, I nodded to Cove.

"I need to take this. Eat whatever you want. I made it for your birthday."

She didn't hide the smile eating up her whole face before I spun and left out the back door, shutting it behind me for some privacy.

I spoke in code, "The bunny has been a bit of a pain in the ass, but nothing I can't handle."

"You're the best for a reason. That was quite a performace you put on at that party."

"I'm just doing my job."

"She was the belle of the ball. You have two days until your honeymoon is over. I'm sure you're beginning to wrap things up on your end?"

"Mm-hmm."

"Great. I'd hate for you to miss your flight home, Jace."

"I've never missed a flight before, William."

"That's why you're the best husband."

He abruptly hung up, and I deeply inhaled, trying to ease the stress of him on my ass and not wanting Cove to see it.

When I returned to the kitchen, she was eating at the dining table. I took a minute to take her in. I could see it in her eyes.

The doubt.

The insecurity.

The sadness for me.

Everything I shared last night continued to weigh heavy on her mind. It was one of the reasons I shut people out. My burdens were mine alone to carry.

There was nothing worse.

I wanted to remember the way she looked at me yesterday, rather than the way she was looking at me now. I had no idea where we went from here. Cove was becoming my biggest weakness and, at the same time, my greatest strength.

So many what-ifs raced through my mind.

So many consequences and scenarios that could happen.

So many fucking choices that could be right or wrong.

Unable to help myself, I reached over and caressed the side of her face, and she leaned into my embrace like she had been waiting for me to do so since the second I walked back into the kitchen.

Her eyes closed, melting into my touch.

The smell and feel of her were all around me, making me burn with desire to claim every last fucking inch of her. I wanted to capture this moment and hold on to it for as long as I could. I wanted to remember her just like this.

For me.

"You make me want to be a better man, bunny."

Her eyes snapped open with so much fucking emotion, it almost knocked me on my ass as she looked deep into my eyes. Her breathing hitched when my thumb pulled on her bottom lip.

Within a second, my hand suddenly moved to grip the back of her neck, and I brought her up toward me. Once she was standing in front of me, I laid more of my cards out on the table for her.

"I talked to Haven this morning."

"They're coming home from their trip, right?"

I nodded.

"Does she know about us?"

"She knows your missing."

"Does she know I'm with you?"

"She knows I'm looking for you. It's only so she wouldn't call the cops to report you missing."

"What about my parents? They haven't—"

"No."

She bowed her head. "Yeah…"

"Look me in the eyes and ask me, Cove."

She did. "What's going to happen? You said you had a week, and that's almost over. If you don't figure it out in the next forty-eight hours, where does that leave me?"

"Today isn't about anything other than your birthday, bunny."

"What does that mean?"

"You're going to get dressed, and we're going out to celebrate."

"Are you serious?"

I smiled, trying to lessen the tension. "Like a bullet to the head."

"You would use that as a metaphor."

I knew there was no coming back from this, but fuck it, I threw caution to the wind. It was her birthday, and I wanted to make it as memorable as I could for her. This week had been hell for her. It was the least I could do after what I was putting her through.

Groaning against her mouth, I rasped, "I'm going to kiss you now."

Her lips parted to say something.

"I'm not asking. I'm telling you."

Before she could reply, I kissed her, beckoning her lips to open for me. They did, releasing a soft moan as she felt my tongue in her mouth. I'd always been a man of few words. To me, actions always spoke much louder and clearer than any sentence could ever provide.

Yet there I was, kissing her like she was mine.

"Jace…" she whispered against my lips. "What's going to happen between us after this?"

"Cove, you already know the answer to that."

"And what if I say no?"

"It doesn't matter."

"So what I want once again doesn't matter?" She pushed off my chest.

"My whole life hasn't mattered to the people who it should have the most. Now am I going to have to add you to that list too?"

I responded with the only thing I could. "Let's just enjoy your birthday today, alright?"

I needed a minute to think, wanting to gather my thoughts.

My emotions.

The impulses she put me through.

My entire life had been built around control.

A schedule.

A routine.

For the first time in my life, I didn't have any of those things when it came to my little sister's best friend.

Once I found my sanity again, I ordered, "Go get ready. We have a long day ahead of us."

Ignoring my request, she countered her own, "It's my birthday, right? That means I get what I want?"

Intrigued about where she was going with this, I took her bait. "Something like that."

"Fine, then I have my own demand for what I want."

I arched an eyebrow, curious where she was going with this. I wish I could tell you I expected what she said next, but I didn't.

Not for one second.

In all one breath, she ordered...

"I want you to take my virginity."

Once again, almost knocking me on my ass.

CHAPTER 24
COVE

Why I expected him to actually answer me was probably one of my dumbest thoughts since he killed Deacon. For a man I was supposed to be madly in love with, I barely thought about him these past few days I was with Jace.

I couldn't believe how things changed so quickly, how fast everything escalated between us, and how much I didn't want it to end. This wasn't a man I only just met—I'd known him for almost my entire life.

He was my first crush, and now he was becoming my first everything. I guess he was making up for lost time of completely taking up residence in my head. My intense feelings for Jace didn't compare to what I felt for whatever his real name was.

There was no comparing the two.

After I was finished getting dressed, I decided it was time for me to take things into my own hands. If I wanted to make him take my virginity, then I needed to give him blue balls to the worst extent.

Grabbing a pair of jean shorts, I cut them up to basically make them daisy dukes and I did the same with my tank top. After looking at my extremely revealing outfit in the floor-length mirror, I decided not to wear a bra with my stark white shirt. Smiling at myself in the mirror, I grabbed the wedge sandals in the closet to accentuate my long legs and finished off my ensemble with light makeup.

"Okay! I'm ready!" I exclaimed, striding into the living room to find Jace sitting on the couch.

He immediately snapped, "What the fuck are you wearing?"

"What?" I played innocent, spinning for him. "Don't you like my outfit?"

"What outfit? You're wearing nothing."

"It's my birthday. I can do what I want."

He growled, fueling my satisfaction.

"You think you have this all planned out, don't you?"

I nodded, proud as fuck.

"Bunny, what am I going to do with you?"

"Well, first… I want to go to a bikini shop."

I thought he was going to kiss me again, and I waited on pins and needles to feel his lips against mine.

He didn't.

Instead, he walked toward me, and each step was more determined than the last.

"Something you want from me?" he taunted.

Asshole.

"Nope." I popped my p, mirroring his expression. "Let's go."

He scoffed out, reaching for me, but I was faster. I darted toward the car and slammed the door in his face.

"You'll pay for that later, Cove."

I leaned into the window, looking deep into his eyes. "I can't wait."

For the next few hours, he treated me like a queen as we enjoyed each other's company until we were at lunch.

Out of nowhere, I blurted, "Is this a date?"

He leaned back into his chair, cocking his head at me.

"It feels like a date." I winked at him. "A very good one by the way."

It was obvious he was fighting his emotions for what he thought was right or wrong between us. It didn't matter what I said, but it was beginning to feel like a huge part of him just wanted to suffer.

To hurt.

As if he was punishing himself for something he couldn't confess to me.

Jace was living in the past, and I had no clue how to pull him out of it or how to set him free from the things that tormented him. It was an endless battle, and I wasn't winning in the least.

He was too guarded.

Too stubborn.

Too everything.

"I know what you're thinking." Setting down my fork, I continued, needing to get my point across. "I've been through a lot for only being nineteen. I know you're twenty years older than me. You lived a whole lifetime before I was even born, but that doesn't mean I can't understand what you've been through. What you're still going through. I'm sure you've seen and done things you're not proud of, but we all have. That's just life, like you keep reminding me life's not fair. You can't keep pushing people away or you're going to end up alone, and I know deep down, you don't want that."

"Cove—"

"Do you have any idea how much your family loves you? You put yourself at risk with what you're doing. What if something goes wrong and you don't make it out alive? You really want to put them through that again?"

He didn't say a word.

"You weren't there to see what it was like for them to live without your mom. She was everything to everyone, and to lose someone so important to all of you destroyed your family for a long time. They don't deserve you putting your life on the line because you're on some crusade to prove something to yourself. When is it going to be enough for you? Don't you want to live a normal life?"

"And what's normal to you, Cove?"

"A family, a wife, maybe even kids?"

"With you?"

"It wouldn't be the worst idea."

"I'm sure Haven would love that."

"As a matter of fact, she would. She's always wanted me to date one of her brothers. It would make us a real family, and we'd be sisters. I can't tell you how many times she's brought this up, hoping it would happen. The night you carried me out of the bar, before we went out with you guys. She was talking about you and me, and I couldn't believe she thought something could actually happen between us. It was like she felt it."

"Jesus, bunny…" he breathed out. "You're nineteen. You have your whole life ahead of you. You're too young to even be considering these things with me or any other man."

"That's where you're wrong. If it wasn't for your family, I honestly don't know where I'd be. I've raised myself. As you know, my parents give two fucks about me. All I've ever wanted was a family of my own. I can't wait to start a life with someone."

"What about college?"

"I'm going to college in the fall." I shrugged. "But I'm a trust fund baby. Money has never been a factor in my decision-making. It's the only thing my parents ever did for me. I like to think it's because they're trying to assuage their guilt for not being parents for me, but I'm great on my own."

"You're impulsive."

"So are you. You're this puzzle I'm desperately trying to put together."

"And why is that?"

Was I really going to tell him?

This was the only thing left for me to say to him. I was going to put my heart on the line more than I already had. I silently prayed it'd be enough.

Taking a deep breath, I admitted for the first time out loud and to him, "It's always been you, Jace. I'm falling in lov—"

"It's called Stockholm Syndrome," he carelessly interrupted.

"Oh yeah?" I argued. "Then how do you explain being my first crush when I was eight?"

Jace

Not many things in life shocked me. I'd seen and experienced it all. But this...

I'd be lying if I said I wasn't surprised by her confession.

She narrowed her sparkling eyes at me with a challenging demeanor. Although, her vulnerability didn't stop me from taking in the glow of her smooth tan skin, the way her hair kept falling around her face, or even the rosy flush of her cheeks.

Her concern.

Her sadness.

The understanding in her eyes.

Cove may have been young, but I could see myself in her. Not having parents made her grow up fast, and I couldn't have been prouder of the woman she became. She was strong, resilient, and didn't back down for anyone.

I needed to know, so I asked, "What happened to that crush?"

She hid back a smile, loving the effect she was having on me.

"It lay dormant until a few days ago."

Neither one of us said anything for a minute until she added, "Are you just going to sit and pretend you don't have feelings for me too? Because I call bullshit, Jace Beckham. If that were true, you wouldn't have touched me from the moment you got me alone."

"You mean taking you to a sex party? That's love to you?"

I was pure.

Innocent.

Naive.

She was the complete opposite of me, and it was part of her allure. I corrupted the angel in my darkness. The worst part was I had no fucking problem in doing so. I wasn't alone anymore—I had her. With the devil on my side, I'd make her mine if I could.

If this were a dream, I'd never want to wake up. Not now, not ever. Her eyes held so much emotion, and her sincere expression was almost hard to follow. I had always been so in tune with what her eyes shared with me, and at that moment, all I could see was her love.

Her devotion.

Her sincerity.

My heart ached at the sight of her. There was no confusion on her behalf, and it wreaked havoc on the pieces left of me. I could physically feel her emotions, and I wanted to keep them forever. I felt her much more than I could have ever imagined. My control was gone, and I wasn't entirely sure if I'd given it over to her or if she'd stolen it from me.

Did it matter?

We stared into each other's eyes, seeing our truths reflecting back at us.

I wouldn't cave.

I couldn't.

Not when I'd end up breaking her.

Or worse…

I'd fucking kill her.

CHAPTER 25
COVE

"I promise to be a very good girl if you tell me where we're going," I baited.

"As much as I would love to see how far you'd take that promise, I'm still not telling you a damn thing."

The rest of our lunch was quiet, and I knew he was mostly thinking about everything I just openly shared with him. This man was a paradox of contractions. From his words to his touch, to how he was going out of his way to make my birthday special for me. I had no idea what he had planned for the rest of the day, but it didn't stop my excitement for what was to come.

When we walked down the beach at Mullet Bay, there was a whole spread for us, blankets, pillows, a cooler, and a picnic basket all stationed perfectly with a hammock.

"I can't believe you did this."

He shrugged. "I just wanted to do something nice for you, so I did."

There was a lot of thought behind his actions today, and I noticed every last one.

"This is really sweet of you."

"You make it easy, bunny."

Once we sat down, I acknowledged, "Thanks for letting me drive the fancy sportscar here."

"I still can't believe I fear for my life when you're in the driver's seat."

"Jace." I smacked his chest. "I'm just a cautious driver."

"You hit a rim on the drive here."

"That curb came out of nowhere."

"Tell that to all the curbs you hit every time you drove Haven's car."

I giggled. "How do you remember that?"

"I remember a lot of things."

"Is this what we're doing today? Taking a walk down memory lane?"

"Is that what you want?"

I nodded. "How about you tell me one of your favorite memories?"

"You really want to go there?"

"Absolutely."

"Cove—"

"It's my birthday. You have to do what I want. Those are the rules. I didn't make them up."

"How convenient for you."

I lay down on my side with my arm supporting my head, eagerly waiting for his response.

"If I tell you, this won't end well for us."

"Try me."

"You're very bossy today."

"You're rubbing off on me."

"Cove, it's not—"

"Nope! No excuses. Tell me." I pouted. "Please."

He sighed, giving in. "It was your senior prom night."

My mouth parted, never expecting him to say that.

"You were coming down the stairs in a soft yellow dress."

I think I stopped breathing.

"You'd pinned your hair to the side of your face and wore more makeup than I'd ever seen you in. I remember thinking it couldn't have been you. You looked so grown up, so fucking beautiful. I was so used to seeing you as my little sister's best friend, and for the first time, I didn't recognize you."

My heart fluttered, and my breathing caught.

"I tried to shake it off, but then my dad asked me to take a picture of the three of you, and I just remember looking through the lens and hesitating for a second. I couldn't take my eyes off you."

"I remember that. You looked annoyed before you gave the camera to Reid. I just thought you were being broody like always." Needing him to get to the point, I questioned, "Why is that a favorite memory of yours?"

My stomach dropped when he declared, "It was the first time I stopped seeing you as Haven's best friend and saw you as a woman."

I lightly gasped, trying to keep my emotions in check.

"That's why I gave the camera over to Reid. I couldn't hide behind it, which is kind of ironic, considering it feels like I've been hiding from everyone for the past twenty years. No one knows who I am, Cove. Nobody knows the things I've done or what I'm capable of."

"That's not true," I stated. "I know you."

"You don't know everything about me."

"So then tell me. What are you hiding from?"

He looked away, breaking our connection. "Let's just enjoy your birthday."

I reluctantly let it go because he grabbed my hand and led me to the hammock. In one swift movement, he laid me on his chest to play with my hair and back.

It was perfect.

He was perfect.

We stayed there with me in his arms for a while. No words were needed.

About an hour later, he stated, "I have one last surprise for you."

I looked up at her, nuzzling his face. "Can I have a hint?" When I felt his breath on my neck, I tingled all over.

In one quick breath, he rasped, "I'm going to make you wet."

My breathing hitched, and my thighs clenched. Of course, he noticed. He grinned against my skin with my heart suddenly beating a mile a minute in the anticipation of what was to come from him.

Especially after what I requested earlier that day.

Was he going to give me what I wanted?

He pulled me off the hammock, leading us to a dock that had a Jet Ski by it.

"You didn't?"

He wickedly grinned, and it was becoming my favorite expression of his. This man was frustrating and charming all at once.

"You want to go for a ride?"

I fervently nodded as excitement took hold of my entire body. This wasn't the wet I wanted, but it was a start.

Jace

I was doing this for her, but I was also doing it for myself. For the first time since Hope, I was happy. Given our circumstances, it didn't make any sense, but I was beginning to understand that maybe we needed one another more than I cared to admit. The look on her face was worth everything I did for her that day.

The crazy thing about it was that I'd willingly give her whatever she wanted to see that expression for the rest of my life.

What was happening to me?

To her?

To us?

I shook away the emotions, focusing on driving the Jet Ski instead. We drove around for hours, laughing.

Smiling.

Truly living in the moment.

Once we were near the bridge, I drove up onto the sand.

"I want to drive."

Before I could tell her no, she straddled my lap.

"I thought you wanted to drive."

"I do."

The minx began rocking her pussy against my cock, and I didn't falter. Gripping the back of her neck, I kissed her as she continued to dry fuck me on the Jet Ski.

Never in a million years did I expect what happened next.

She pushed me back, quickly jumping off my lap to run under the bridge giggling.

"What are you doing?"

"Taking what I want like you should."

Before I could contemplate what she meant, she turned with her back facing me and started untying her top.

Nice and slow.

At first, I thought she was toying with me. Readily showing me how wrong I was. Little by little, I crumpled to the ground while she revealed more of her creamy bare skin. I devoured every inch of her flesh as she exposed herself to me. Giving her control was my first mistake.

I tried not to gawk, but fuck me… I couldn't help it.

From the back of her thighs, I drank her in as she dropped her top into the sandy water under the bridge. Her narrow, slender waist was just as arousing, rendering me fucking speechless. I was consumed by the fact that I was the first man ever to see her this way.

Only making me want her that much more.

She shook out her long blond hair, and it cascaded all the way down her back. I licked my lips, my mouth suddenly becoming dry. The minute she cupped her tits, I knew I was done for.

There would be no coming back from this.

From *her.*

From *us.*

Her tantalizing bright-blue eyes glanced back at me over her shoulder, and I couldn't gather a fucking thought. She was stunning, with her hair flowing loosely around her gorgeous face. Although it was her eyes that captured my attention the most. I'd seen Cove in all forms.

A girl.

A woman.

Now there she was, proving to me she would get what she demanded. I had no idea how things escalated so quickly. Her demeanor took on a whole different persona, showing a side of her I didn't know existed.

Her eyes glazed over with a heady allure. Appearing alive and vibrant, thriving in my direction. My head spun with where she was going with this, but as much as it caught me off guard, it turned me the fuck on.

With a heated glare, I watched her hands glide down her waist in slow motion to untie her bikini bottoms. Not once did her gaze leave mine, loving the reaction she purposely stirred inside me.

From my mind down to my fucking cock.

CHAPTER 26
COVE

I grabbed the string of my bottoms, loosening one before the other. His eyes widened, realizing what I was about to do.

"Bunny," he rasped in a tone that drove me wild, fueling my desire to show him there was more to me than met the eye or the pedestal he was adamant to keep me on.

This was the perfect opportunity to show him what I was made of. Not thinking twice about it, I teasingly tossed them in his direction. We were alone, not a person in sight, as if this moment was meant to be here.

I was never the girl who wanted her first time to be nice and gentle on a bed. Maybe that was another reason it never felt right with Deacon or whatever the hell his name was.

I always knew I wanted my first time to be wild.

Adventurous.

Completely spontaneous.

And Jace was the man who could give me all three.

I cocked my head to the side, flashing him a provocative look. His breathing caught, giving me what I longed for.

His desire.

Need.

And cock.

Was only for me.

With a hungry and greedy regard, he engulfed me with a single stare. One look drove me to the brink of insanity as I anticipated his hands on me.

"Bunny..." he warned in a shaky tone. "You don't know what you're doing."

"I know exactly what I'm doing. I told you what I wanted for my birthday. It's you, Jace. It's always been you."

In three strides, he was in my face and grabbing my legs to wrap around his waist. In a flash, my back was up against one of the poles of the bridge.

I was panting.

He was panting.

We were lost in each other.

We locked eyes, suddenly realizing the compromising position we'd rapidly found ourselves in.

My nipples were flat against his chest.

My arms were around his neck.

My wet pussy was against his hard dick, causing me to suck in another breath.

"This what you want, Cove?"

"Yes..."

He slammed his lips onto mine. Our mouths moved against one another, taking what the other craved in a frenzy of passion and longing.

"Fuck…" he exclaimed against my mouth. "This isn't right. I shouldn't be doing this. You don't belong to me."

"Just be with me, Jace. I'll beg if I have to. I know how much you love having me at your mercy."

He chuckled, sliding his tongue past my lips.

The strength.

The pull.

It was inevitable.

There was no reason to deny it anymore.

The water splashed at our feet, making this much more intense between us. I savored his taste and the feel of him between my legs.

Our chests heaved profusely.

Our emotions ran wild and out of control, but somehow, they were still in sync.

His dark and daunting eyes aimed a passionate, crazed stare. The man in front of me wasn't the Jace I knew. This man had lost all control to me, and I couldn't have been more thrilled to have won this battle.

He surrendered.

His white flag was up.

And I knew how hard that must have been for him.

"You're the sweetest thing." He laid his forehead against mine. "I don't deserve this. I don't deserve you."

"Maybe that's the point of us." I kissed him. "We're here to heal the broken people inside us."

His eyes widened, taking in what I was wholeheartedly expressing.

I had nowhere to go.

I could barely move.

My body was on fire.

There wasn't an inch of me that didn't throb for him, that didn't ache for him, that didn't want or need him.

I craved his touch.

His words.

His love more now than ever before.

Kissing me deeply, he groaned, "I want you more than I've ever wanted anything in this world."

I beamed as he once again claimed my mouth. At that moment, in that second, time just stood still for us. There was no two days left of this week. No enemies. No family. No past.

It was just us.

"You want me, bunny?"

I eagerly nodded, my core seizing up. Nervous and excited all at once.

"Here? Like this?"

"Yes."

He made a noise from the back of his throat, adding fuel to the flames burning inside me.

Within seconds, my body reacted. I started to rock my hips on his cock, which earned me yet another growl and only heightened my desire for him. Higher and higher, I rose until finally—he lost all control.

Handing it right over to me.

Everything was about to change between us again, and I couldn't have been more ready for it.

He was mine.

I was his.

End of story.

Jace

"I can still taste your sweet little cunt in my mouth."

In one swift movement, I placed her feet on the watery sand and dropped to my knees. Roughly gripping her thighs, I thrust her pussy toward my mouth.

She gasped a heady breath.

I took my time, savoring the feel of her silky thighs against my lips and unshaven face. Inch by inch, I made her pant above me as I made my way toward her pussy, working her into a frenzy.

Kissing.

Licking.

Biting.

I inhaled her addicting scent of arousal mixed with the sweet smell of her cunt. Finally, I ended my fucking torture for us both and kissed her clit, fighting the urge to suck it into my mouth and bury my face between her legs.

"Beg me, bunny," I growled. "Beg me to make you come." I continued my assault on every sensitive spot except where we both wanted my tongue the most.

"Please, Jace… please make me come…"

I thrust my tongue into the opening of her pussy.

"Jace…" she purred, fisting her hand in my hair.

I glided my tongue up to her clit and sucked it into my starving mouth, giving it one soft lick before I peered up at her again with a ravenous glare.

"You want me to fuck you with my tongue?"

"Yes…"

I did just that.

Her eyes closed, and her head fell back, grinding her hips in a back-and-forth motion against my lips and tongue. I devoured her pussy from the inside, out. Her hand tightly clutched onto my hair again, almost like she was trying to rip it the fuck out. Making my cock throb so hard against my swim trunks. Licking her juices, I built up her wetness with each lap of my tongue.

Getting her nice and ready to take my cock.

"Oh God…"

She came so fucking hard, dripping down my chin. I didn't stop. I was a crazed man. I made her come in my mouth until she screamed out my name, begging for mercy.

Over and over again.

When her legs gave out on her from my relentless pursuit of her come, I stood and took her with me to once again wrap her legs around my waist. Backing her up against one of the poles, I pulled down my shorts, kissing her long and deep as I fisted my cock. Water splashed around our feet.

All of a sudden, it hit me hard and fast.

She must have noticed because she revealed, "I'm on the Depo shot."

Breathing out a sigh of relief that she was on birth control, I spoke with conviction. "I'm going to ruin you."

"Promise?" she repeated.

I caged her in with my arms around her face, gripping the back of her neck, not wanting to lose our connection.

"Don't close your eyes. I want you to look at me as I fuck you raw for the first time."

She moaned in response.

I didn't want to hurt her. I should have fingered her first to get her used to the feeling of something inside her, but I was a selfish fuck. I wanted to feel her for the first time on my cock.

"I don't know how to do gentle, Cove."

"I don't want it soft. I just want you in whatever way you want to take me. Claim me. Mark me. Make me remember this moment for the rest of my life, Jace. Be with me how you want."

I didn't have to be told twice. In one hard, demanding thrust, I was deep inside her.

She huffed out somewhere between pain and ecstasy.

She was warm.

Wet.

Tight as fuck.

"Jesus Christ, bunny, I'm going to break you."

Lighting my match, she repeated, "Promise?"

"I fucking swear it."

Her gaze held so many emotions I couldn't begin to describe. Her arms held me tighter as I began thrusting in and out of her. She made me feel whole and complete for the first time in my life. I couldn't have been more wrong about Hope.

It was Cove.

She was mine.

But was I hers?

The expression on her face was my undoing. I reached down and started rubbing her overly sensitive clit with my fingers, and her pussy constricted around my shaft. I realized she was beginning to enjoy what I was giving.

I made love to her the only way I knew how, never feeling this with anyone before. I felt every last inch of her wrapped around me as our bodies tangled together against the pole.

I cherished every sound.

Every touch.

Every sensation she stirred within my heart and what was left of my soul.

I kissed her, savoring our skin-on-skin contact. She was everything I ever wanted and didn't know I could have.

"Fuck," I groaned, rotating my hips.

I got lost inside her for what felt like hours, knowing this wouldn't be enough. She was throbbing, coming apart.

We were both on the verge of going over, and I wanted to do it together. My fingers rubbed faster and harder, manipulating her clit.

"Yeah, bunny ... just like that ... come for me... give it to me."

She did just that, coming down my balls.

Two more thrusts and I was right there with her. Growling from within my chest, I fucked my seed deep inside her.

Immediately knowing...

I was falling in love with her.

And what I had to do next.

CHAPTER 27
COVE

I woke up the next morning to Jace ordering, "You need to get dressed."

He was already standing by the bedroom door, wearing his clothes.

"Good morning to you too," I greeted, immediately picking up his tone.

In the blink of an eye, he was back to the cold and calloused man. It was like what happened between us yesterday was an illusion. For a second, I thought I imagined last night, but the soreness of my core and body proved otherwise.

"Are we going somewhere?" I asked in an anxiety-stricken state of mind.

"Yes," he replied.

Our eyes never wavered from one another, captivated in each other's stares.

"Is everything alright?"

"Nothing's ever alright."

"Are we—"

"I'm a killer, Cove. The sooner you realize that. The easier this will be between us."

"You mean the easier it will be on you?"

"Bunny, I know who I am. It's you who doesn't."

Thinking about it for a second, I rasped, "Please don't be like this." I was on the verge of tears.

"Cove," he sternly spoke. "Get dressed. I'll be waiting for you downstairs."

He turned to leave, but stopped dead in his tracks when I declared, "You're better than this, Jace."

He stayed froze where he stood, not bothering to turn around.

Which only gave me more ammunition to keep going. "What if I told you I'm in love with you? Would you still be trying to push me away right now?"

I didn't know what I expected out of him, but it still hurt like a bitch when he didn't say a word.

No response.

No emotion.

Nothing.

All he did was walk away from me with my heart pouring out for him.

I stayed there, rationalizing the abrupt change in his demeanor. The man with me yesterday was long gone, and in his place was the contract killer I kept encountering.

I tried to figure out where he was taking me and what would happen next before I jumped out of bed. I couldn't help but remember that I slept in his arms last night and now he was pretending like none of what happened yesterday mattered anymore.

Once I took a shower and brushed my teeth, I felt much more at ease.

However, I knew whatever occurred next wasn't going to be easy by any means. Despite sleeping in his arms, it didn't change his demeanor. He was again the soldier, hiding behind his uniform.

I dressed in jean shorts, a tank top, and sandals, leaving my hair down with mascara, blush, and lip gloss. I knew I took longer than he probably expected, but he didn't say anything when I walked into his living room ready to go.

He drove us in awkward silence as I craved for him to put his hand on my thigh like he had all day prior. I longed for him to comfort me with a touch, a gesture, wishing what transpired last night would have changed the outcome of this morning.

One thing I was sure of, I knew he wouldn't hurt me, at least not physically. Now emotionally and mentally was a much different story. He just stared out the windshield, rubbing his fingers across his lips, lost in his own thoughts, in his own demons. In his own world like I'd never seen before.

The car ride could have lasted a minute, an hour, or a few days. Time just seemed to stand still again but not like yesterday. It felt as though every second that passed between us was another moment in time for him. It felt like I was the hell he constantly lived in.

Without thinking, I reached over and placed my hand on his, lacing our fingers together before giving him a reassuring squeeze. His eyes quickly darted at my kind gesture as if he was waiting for something I didn't understand. His hand remained lax, and he didn't return my sentiment. After a few seconds, he looked back up, not giving my affection any more consideration.

Too many plaguing thoughts consumed him, which scared me in a way it hadn't yet. Whatever was about to happen was going to hurt badly and there was no denying the emotions wreaking havoc all around us.

We drove to what appeared to be a park that was surrounded by beautiful trees and greenery. My heart sped up as we neared our final destination. Tree after tree whipped by the black tinted windows, causing shadows in our path as they started to blur in the background and fade into the distance.

Jace didn't remove my hand, but he also didn't acknowledge it. My heart pounded out of my chest, and I swear he could hear it, feel it, sense it.

As soon as he parked the car, he opened the door and exited. I stayed seated for another moment, trying to gather my bearings for what was still to come. He knew I had questions attacking the forefront of my mind rapidly, yet he didn't try to comfort me in the least.

Yesterday proved one thing, and one thing only. I was his weakness, and I wasn't aware if it was a good or bad thing yet. I decided I needed to put on my big girl panties and ignore the ache in my chest trying to overpower me.

Inhaling a deep breath, I stepped out of the passenger seat, immediately peering up at him. I searched his eyes for the answers I desperately sought but he showed me nothing of the man who was so caring, loving and attentive the day before.

It was obvious he didn't want to provide me with any ease or reassurance. That's not what this was about, it was the exact opposite, and I understood that instantly with his ominous stare and hard as fuck composure he was pulling on me.

"Come on." He nodded, leading the way deeper into the garden.

He walked like a man on a mission.

Like a man on death row.

Almost like he was walking through the valley of the shadow of death, and I was simply along for the ride, hanging on for dear life. A life I still wanted with him. Today's outcome wouldn't change my love for him.

He trudged until there were no more steps to take.

Until the doubt.

The fear.

Were alive and present, standing by our sides.

"Jace, what's going on?" I asked, unable to hold back my worry. "Why are we here?"

He didn't falter, putting an end to the fantasy I had created in my head.

"Her name was Hope."

I narrowed my eyes at him, listening intently to what he was about to share with my heart in my throat.

"She was my best friend's fiancée." He paused to let his words sink in. "Before I killed him too."

I jerked back. "What?"

"You heard me."

I shuddered, sucking in a breath.

"This is my life, Cove. People die around me, some of them from my bare hands while others were from my gun and rifle. My hands are covered in blood. I'm surprised you can't see it, but I know you can feel it."

I stepped toward him, but he stepped back.

"I know what you do is dangerous, but I also know there's a reason for it, so tell me what happened. I want the whole story."

He openly shared, "He saved my life in the line of duty, and before I could thank him, I killed him. How's that for a story?"

"Jace…"

"I brought her here. To the exact spot you're standing in right now."

"Why?"

"She was the only one who understood what it was like to lose him. She was also the only one who understood what it was like to lose myself in the process."

"Does that mean you were together?"

"Not in an intimate way, but that didn't matter to me."

"Then in what way were you to each other?"

"It started off as letters and turned into something else entirely. I told her things I've never told anyone. She was easy to talk to, and I never had that before. I lost my mom a year prior, and I never mourned her. I didn't grieve her death. Instead, I lost myself in my career until she wrote me one day, and we began our relationship."

"So what happened?"

"I took care of her and sent her money. I even got her an apartment for her and her unborn son."

I lightly sucked in a breath. "She was pregnant?"

"Yeah. He was so excited to be a father. He talked about Hope all the time. He was almost fucking done, Cove. It was almost time for him to live a normal life with the family he always wanted."

I swallowed hard. "I'm so sorry, Jace."

"He begged me to kill him, pleaded with me to take his life. He wanted to die with honor, and it was the only thing I could do for him at the moment. I promised to take care of Hope and his son, and I did. I followed through, and in the process, I thought I fell in love with her."

I winced. Now that was the hardest part to hear.

"But it wasn't love. It was just trauma bonding. It's exactly the same reason you feel like you're in love with me."

"Don't!" I shouted harder than I intended to. "That's not fair. My feelings aren't like yours. This isn't the same situation."

"I don't fucking love you, Cove! Do you hear me? You're nothing but my little sister's best friend! You mean nothing to me! Do you understand me? Can you fucking hear me for once?"

"Stop it! Don't do this!"

"Do what? Tell you the truth?" He snidely grinned. "I'll tell you what, though, your virgin-tight pussy was nice to fuck."

I slapped him across the face as hard as I could. My hand stung, but it was nowhere near what my heart felt with his brutally cruel statement. I didn't hold back. I went at him.

Shoving.

Hitting.

Pounding my fists into his chest.

I didn't pay any mind to the throbbing pain shooting through my hands and tearing through my body at the same time. My mind urged me to keep going. However, my heart pleaded with me to stop.

"You don't mean that! I know you don't mean that!"

He didn't try to fight me off. He let me attack him without blocking any of my advances. Almost like he knew he deserved it for purposely trying to hurt me, ruining and breaking me like he promised.

"Why are you like this?! Why can't you just let me in?!"

He gripped my wrists, holding me in place in front of him and I didn't stop.

I couldn't.

"You want me to hate you?" I spewed with my emotions getting the best of me. "Well then here! I'll fucking say it! I hate you, Jace Beckham! I fucking hate you so much! I hate the way you make me feel! I hate the way I can't stop thinking about you!" Tears filled my eyes. "I hate that you broke my eight-year-old heart! I made you that red velvet cake with my nanny, asshole! Knowing it was your favorite! And all you did was treat me like shit! Exactly like you are right now!" The tears slid down the sides of my face; there was no controlling those either.

"I gave you my bunny! It was my favorite stuffed animal, and I gave it to you! Only for you to toss it away like it meant nothing when it meant everything to me!"

I thrashed my body around, trying to break free from the hold he had on me. I couldn't breathe, drowning deeper into my despair. It was one of my worst memories, and I was reliving it all over again because of him and his selfishness.

He yanked me toward him, inches away from his lips to warn, "You want to know why I can't let you in? I'll fucking tell you! The last woman I let into my life stood where you are right now… happy, hopeful, filled with so much fucking life!"

His words had a chokehold on me, strangling me harder, faster, to the point that it felt as if I wouldn't survive it. I thought I knew everything about him, but I couldn't have been more wrong.

At that exact moment, he revealed, "She was shot by one of my enemies! Do you hear me now? Are you listening? It was a fucking sniper that I've been searching for ever since! Is that what you wanted to hear? She died right where you're standing. Can you feel her? Because I sure as fuck can!"

I would remember this split second for the rest of my life. Out of all the times I wanted him to tell me the truth, I never expected it would end me too.

"She died in my fucking arms, Cove!"

I gasped, stumbling back as soon as the last word left his mouth. Except it wasn't from what he finally confessed to me after all this time.

No.

I fell back from the bullet…

That just shot me in my chest.

CHAPTER 28
JACE

"**N**OOOO!" I heard the desperation in my voice, reliving my worst nightmare all over again.

I watched a bullet lodge into Cove's chest from what could only be the mark of a skilled sniper somewhere hidden once again.

She staggered back before she collapsed into my arms, coughing up blood.

"No! No! No! No! No!"

I couldn't breathe.

I couldn't fucking breathe.

Cove wasn't smiling.

She wasn't laughing.

She was just bleeding out profusely.

My vision tunneled. All the blood drained from my face as her blood drenched my skin, my heart, and what was left of my fucking soul.

Our eyes locked as I shattered with guilt, with pain, with nothing but hatred for the man I'd become.

"Somebody help me!" I shouted loud enough to break glass. "Somebody please fucking help me! Cove, Cove, Cove... stay with me, bunny. Stay fucking with me..."

I gasped for air, pulling out my cell phone from my pocket to dial 911.

A man started running toward us, already on his phone, yelling at them about our location and how she was bleeding out and dying in my arms.

"You're okay, bunny... you're okay..."

Her blood poured through my fingers, soaking my hands, my body, my entire being. No matter how much pressure I applied, it wouldn't stop.

So much fucking blood.

My eyes frantically searched for something to apply more pressure to her gaping hole. My hands weren't enough to control the bleeding pouring out of her.

The stranger who was helping us was suddenly above me. "Here, man!!" He threw off his shirt, hanging it to me.

Without hesitation, I grabbed it and applied as much pressure as I could next to her heart. I struggled to keep my shit together, but my sanity, my heart, every last part of me shattered around us, mixing in with her blood.

She was coughing.

Wheezing.

Her body seized uncontrollably with every forced breath that escaped her lips.

"Cove... stay with me... just stay with me... listen to my voice... stay with my voice... okay?" I coaxed with trembling lips and unsteady eyes and composure.

My body shook just as badly as hers was.

"It's okay. You're going to be just fine, bunny. Do you hear me? You're going to be fine. The ambulance is coming. You need to stay with me. Please just stay with me." I sucked in air with my desperation. "Just look at me, Cove. I'm right here. I'm right fucking here with you, and I'm not going anywhere. Please… please don't do this to me… I'm begging you…"

Her fluttering eyes suddenly trapped my gaze. She showed me how much she did in fact love me. For the first time in what felt like forever, tears fell out of my eyes, and I prayed…

"Please, God… please don't do this to me… please…" I shook, shuddering, my voice breaking.

"Jace… am… I… dying?"

"Shhh… save your breath." Unable to hold back the fear in my voice, I ordered, "You stay with me! Do you hear me? Do you understand me? You fucking stay with me, Cove!"

She whimpered in pain as I held her petite frame, which seemed smaller at that moment.

Tighter.

Harder.

I provided the only comfort I could.

With my words.

My touch.

My entire being was dying right along with her.

"You're tough, Cove. You've always been a strong woman."

She sucked in air that wasn't available for the taking.

"You fight! You fucking fight for me! For us! You're my family, bunny. You've always been my family."

She sluggishly nodded. "Pleassse… telllll themmm I love themmm…"

"I don't have to tell them! You will! You're going to be fine. I promise you. Please fight for me!"

The stranger informed, "They're a minute away."

I nodded, never taking my eyes off her. "I can't lose you. Do you hear me, Cove? I can't fucking lose you too!"

My tears fell on her face.

Our pain mixed as one, entwined through the past and present.

The good, the bad.

My darkness, her light.

I shut my eyes, choking back the sobs but opening them just as quickly, not wanting to miss a second with her.

With us.

"I… loveee… youuuu… G.I. Joeeee…"

"No! No! No! Don't you do this! Don't you say goodbye to me! This is not goodbye! Not like this! Don't you leave me! Don't you dare fucking leave me! I won't be able to survive it this time! I won't!"

Heart-wrenching sobs escaped my throat, the kind I didn't know existed, feeling as though I was bleeding tears. I held her closer to my heart, hoping she'd hear it beating for her.

"Do you understand what I'm saying? Do you hear me?"

I broke down, my chest locking up, hyperventilating from bawling so fucking hard. My eyes blurred with tears, barely allowing me to see her beautiful face as my lungs caved in on me. I was suffocating in her.

In everything she ever meant to me.

"I'm begging you… don't leave me…"

My chest heaved, rising and falling with each rigid breath, with each beat of my heart, with each word that escaped my lips. I held her, trying to hold on to our lives together, to our memories, to the future I wanted with her more than anything.

I had to shut my eyes.

My chest burned so badly.

I didn't know if I could ever breathe again.

Her body started to convulse. This time worse than before. Blood gurgled out of her mouth, slowly drowning in her distress while her eyes fluttered to remain open and maintain her focus on me and my distress.

"NOOOOOO! Look at me, bunny! Look at me, Cove! Don't close your eyes! Please don't close your eyes! You need to stay with me. Please, Cove! Just fucking stay with me!"

It felt as if her end was near, and another one of my worst fucking nightmares was about to come true. Her eyes began to roll to the back of her head while a terrified expression marred her beautiful face.

I feared for everything at that moment, but mostly, I feared for the life we might never have together.

"Oh God! No! Please, God, no! Please! Don't do this to me!" I gripped the back of her neck and got right in her face. "Look at me! Fucking look at me, Cove!"

She did with hazy, distant eyes.

I didn't hesitate to tell her the truth.

All of my truths.

"I love you, Cove! I fucking love you! I'm yours! Do you hear me? Can you feel me? I love you with every last part of me. Please… please… don't do this to me… Fight for me… fight for us… fight for my family…"

Her body went lax, and her eyes rolled to the back of her head.

"NOOOOOO! NO! NO!" I screamed until my throat burned and my chest ached. Bawling to the point of immense pain. "NO! NO! NO! PLEASE, GOD, NO!"

Before I could perform CPR, her body was lifted into the air and away from me.

"Sir, you need to move," one of the paramedics demanded.

I didn't even hear them approach.

"We need to help her!"

The rest proceeded in slow motion for what felt like the hundredth time in my life. Paramedics filled the vacant space. I swear I blinked and the defibrator paddles were trying to shock her body back to life.

"One, two, three, clear."

Her chest jolted.

"One, two, three, clear."

Her chest jumped again.

"One, two, three, clear."

I was there, but I wasn't.

I was having an out-of-body experience. My mind was protecting itself from the consequences of my choices. I stayed there watching my life flash before my eyes until they said the only two words I truly dreaded to hear.

"Call it," the paramedic said.

Everything went dark around me because Cove Noel…

Died at 11:35 a.m.

CHAPTER 29
JACE

"Fuck this shit!"

I tore the defibrillator pads from the paramedic's hands. I'd seen this performed several times from being in the military and constantly in the war zone.

"Sir! What are you doing?" the EMT questioned.

I didn't hesitate for a second. Increasing the voltage of shock on the machine, I placed the defibrillator pads on her chest and shocked her my damn self before checking her pulse.

Nothing.

"Sir! You cannot—"

"The fuck I can't!" Putting my mouth on hers, I began CPR since I had training for it. After two breaths, I started thirty chest compressions with my hands on the center of her chest.

Ten.

"Come on, Cove!"

"Sir," the paramedic snapped. "Please…"

Fifteen.

"Don't do this to me, Cove!"

Twenty.

Someone tried to grab me, and with one glare their way, I spewed, "Touch me again, and I'll fucking kill you."

He put his arms in the air in a surrendering gesture.

Twenty-five.

"Come on, bunny. Haven needs you!"

Thirty.

"I fucking need you!"

I grabbed the pads, shocking her again. With bile rising in the back of my throat, I checked her pulse at the same time the machine stated, "Rhythm detected."

While I simultaneously announced, "She has a pulse!" Inhaling a deep breath, I kissed all over her face. "Fuck, bunny… don't ever do that to me again."

My indescribable relief was immediate. My heart started urgently pounding against my chest as another unsettling feeling churned deep in my stomach. Something about this attack didn't feel right to me. This didn't make any sense, and I wasn't foolish enough to think this wasn't an inside job.

My eyes searched Cove's face for I don't know what, eyeing her up and down. I fought this internal battle to break down.

To fall apart.

The agony was taking ahold of me.

I focused on the relief that she was still alive instead, giving me the strength to hold it together to find the truth of who was behind this and why. A war raged inside me. At the end of this, I'd still have Cove, and it was the only thing getting me through the rest of the day.

For the next few hours were straight out of hell. After surgery, they transferred her to the ICU. The doctor wanted to keep her sedated until she was stabilized, which wouldn't be for another day or two.

The next thing I knew, I was sitting in her room, leaning back into the chair with my head against the wall. My legs were spread out in front of me, and my arms were crossed over my chest.

Fucking waiting.

The chain of events in the past few months led up to this place in time, and soon, the moment of truth would be knocking on my door, ready to barge the fuck in whether I wanted it to or not.

I let the staff handle their protocol, answering the necessary questions. Since she was a target, I had all her medical files and thank God for that. They were able to do whatever protocol they needed in order for her to wake up.

I couldn't believe her parents weren't immediately flying in when the hospital called them with the news. My mind was fucking blown on how much they really didn't give a shit about her. I guess they were content enough with the fact that I was there for her and that my father and Haven were flying in.

My mind ran wild with thought after thought of who could be behind this and why they were putting me through this twice.

In the same location.

With the same attack.

Except with this one, they didn't take two lives this time.

I racked my brain on how this was synced. On what pieces of the puzzle Cove filled.

Why her?

Why Hope?

My entire life flashed before my eyes like a goddamn movie reel that I couldn't pause or stop. It felt like I'd been sitting there for days, but it was only a few hours. I thought about what went down, playing it over in my mind like a broken record on repeat.

I would never be able to forget her blood on my hands.

Her words.

Her pain.

Her death.

I got out of my chair a few times, pacing her room. I tried to shake off my demons that afflicted my mind. It raced with ongoing thoughts, with guilt, and the shame from all the shit I put the people I loved the most through.

The more I thought about it, the less it made sense to me. All the memories faded when I heard footsteps coming down the hall. Then all of a sudden, the man I least expected entered her room from out of nowhere.

I jerked back, taking him in.

"She's prettier in person." He nodded to her sleeping form on the hospital bed.

"What are you doing here, William?"

"I came to see the damsel in distress."

I narrowed my eyes at him, confused by the turn of events.

"We need to talk. Let's go up on the roof and let Sleeping Beauty rest."

Once we were alone on the rooftop, I asked, "What the fuck are you doing here?"

"What's with the tone?"

"You've never shown up on any of my missions, so I'll ask again. What the fuck are you doing here?"

He scoffed out a chuckle. "I just wanted to see how my best killer was doing. Is that a crime?"

My eyebrows pinched together. "How did you even know we were here?"

"I have eyes everywhere, Jace."

"You've never had eyes on me."

"Cove is different from any other target you've had in the past."

"You don't know a fucking thing, William."

"I know you've gone soft for her."

"Again, you don't know a fucking thing."

"If you didn't, you wouldn't have saved her life. Especially since your time is almost up with her and you have yet to figure out who's after you. It's been almost eleven years since Hope. The clock is ticking. You remember that day, don't you?"

With him standing there in front of me, my mind flew back to another place and time, and I had no control over it.

It was raining as I stood over Hope's freshly buried grave. Her funeral was that afternoon, and I couldn't leave her side. Memories of my mother's burial played out as if it were happening again.

"I'm so fucking sorry, Hope. I don't know what else I can say to you to grant you peace, but I pray that you're with Tony. That the three of you are together again, and I was just the stepping stone to get you to him. I hope you're finally a family, the one you both always wanted."

Bending down, I grabbed some dirt and poured it on her grave.

"I'm so fucking sorry."

I didn't even hear him approach as an unfamiliar voice asked, "You want revenge?"

I peered up, locking eyes with a man I'd never seen before.

"Because I can give you that and so much more."

All in one breath, I replied, "I'm listening."

"I'm in the presence of the best sniper in the world. Your reputation precedes you."

"What's it to you?"

"I know who you are, Jace Beckham. Navy SEAL Elite Forces, military ID number 417-85-0212 EF. It's nice to finally meet you."

I zeroed in on him. "What do you want?"

"You on my team."

"What the hell does that mean?"

"It means, I can open a whole new world for you that nobody has to know about and in return, you can get what you really want and can't say out loud."

"And what's that?"

With one word, he gave me the future I desperately yearned for.

"Revenge."

"How?"

"You come work for me. I have contacts, intel, connections you could only dream of."

"Work for what?"

He smiled. "As a contract killer."

No good could come of this, but I didn't care.

I was broken.

Battered.

Beat the fuck down.

He was right. All I wanted was vengeance on who killed Hope and her unborn child. I wouldn't be able to rest until I found her shooter. I desperately needed to know why her...

Why me?

Who did I fuck over?

I made so many enemies during my career that I couldn't fathom who would want me to pay for the ongoing sins I committed.

My life had turned into one big devastation.

The truth was, whoever was her sniper attacker, they didn't want me dead.

No.

All they wanted was…

My wrath.

CHAPTER 30
JACE

There was always that one moment in life when you had a second of clarity. When all you could see was the truth hidden in plain sight. I'd tried to find Hope's killer for the past ten years, only to come up empty.

Why now?

Why today?

Why Cove?

It wasn't until William coaxed, "It's ironic, don't you think?"

"What's that?"

He arched an eyebrow. "Bunny and sweet pea were both shot in the same place."

BOOM.

My life turned into complete transparency, bracing myself for what was to come out this encounter. I tried to keep calm, but I could barely fucking stand.

I saw all his darkest secrets.

All the pain he inflicted.

My hand fisted at my sides. "How did you know Tony's nickname for Hope, William?"

He didn't bat an eye.

There was no movement.

No reaction.

No emotion.

For the first time in what felt like an eternity of trying to figure out the truth, I saw right through him.

"Jace…" he warned, fully aware I was onto him. "Don't let your emotions get the best of you. I trained you better than that."

"You didn't answer my question."

"I told you. I have eyes everywhere. You more than anyone knows that."

"Bullshit! You son of a bitch! You wouldn't have information like that!" Moving on autopilot, I walked toward him. "You have one minute to tell me the truth, or I'll shoot you right between the eyes."

"Jace, you're being impulsive, son."

"I'm not your fucking son."

"I. Made. You."

"Forty seconds."

"You'd be nothing without me."

"Thirty-five."

"I taught you everything you know! Everything! Look at this life I've given you!"

"Twenty-five."

"You don't know what you're thinking. You're exhausted, and you're not seeing reason."

"Fifteen."

"Enough with the dramatics! How dare you question me? Who the fuck do you think you are?"

"Five. Four. Three. Two. One."

Before I got the last number out, we both had our guns aimed at each other's foreheads, but I was quicker and younger. My fist collided with his jaw in one swift movement, and his head whooshed back, taking half his body with him.

He stumbled, and I used his own momentum against him. Quickly, I snatched his Glock out of his grasp and then aimed both of them at his head.

Through a clenched jaw, I spewed, "Don't fuck with me, old man."

He swallowed hard, glaring me up and down.

"Now tell me the truth. Why?"

Despite the trepidation in his eyes, he replied, "Tony was my brother."

I jerked back from the impact of his confession.

"At first, I wanted revenge against you for letting him die on your watch, but then... I just wanted you. You are the fucking best and it didn't take me long to figure that out. Hope was the only way I could get you, and Cove was the only way I could keep you."

"You motherfucker!"

"Fuck you, Jace! You'd be nothing without me!"

"Why weren't you at his funeral?"

"Our father remarried and left me behind since I was much older than Tony. Besides, I was always the blacksheep. Tony was the solider. I wasn't there, but that doesn't mean I didn't fucking love him!"

I desperately tried to calm my emotions, keeping my anger in check.

Needing to know, I roared, "Hope makes sense, but Cove doesn't. She was barely in my life. Why would you go after her to begin with?"

"She wasn't initially my target. Your sister was."

I saw red.

Bright. Fucking. Red.

"But then she got with her boyfriend, and it was too many tracks to cover, so I waited until another opportunity arose to get your attention. When I realized she had a best friend, and how close Cove was to your family, I shifted gears. I implanted Deacon into her life. He was always working for me."

"What did he know?"

"I told him I thought you were a traitor, and I needed information on you."

"You set me up. You told me Deacon was one of my enemies that I needed to take out!"

"It was the only way you'd take Cove. I had to set her up to look like a mission and the next target to you. It was the only way to get her here with you."

"Jesus... how did I not see this?"

"You didn't fucking want to!"

"All this because I wanted out?"

"You're the best, Jace, and I'll do anything to keep you."

"You motherfucker!"

I didn't waver. Gripping the front of his suit jacket, I slammed his back up against the concrete wall behind him. He hit it with a hard thud, knocking the wind out of him for a second. I never took my eyes off his while I lay into him.

He deserved every blow to his body.

Every punch to his face.

Every wound I wanted to stab into him.

No damage could ever compare to what he put me through or what I lost in the process of trying to find myself. Because of him. This piece of shit made my life a living, breathing hell.

"You piece of shit!" I snarled, punching him in the stomach and then again in the ribs.

Another hit to the side of his face.

An uppercut to his jaw, making him instantly taste blood.

I hurled his body across the room, leaving nothing but destruction in my path.

"Why aren't you fighting back, huh?"

He staggered to his feet, wiping the blood off his face with the back of his arm. That was all it took for me to be over to him in two strides, punching him in the face again.

"I fucking hate you!" I hit him in the side of his stomach. "Did you think I wouldn't have figured it out? Your attacks were too personal, and it made you sloppy! All your training! All your knowledge! All your fucking contacts can't save you from me!"

I pounded a few more blows to his ribs. He bent over, gasping for air. I picked him back up, slamming him against another wall behind him. I held up his lax body, shoving him harder against it.

He chuckled. "You can't kill me, and you know it. If you did, you'd make more enemies for yourself. I'm untouchable, Jace. It's what makes me your fucking boss."

"Listen to me because I'm only going to say it once, motherfucker." He shoved him into the wall. "Are you listening?"

He weakly nodded.

"I'm done."

His gaze amplified.

"Do you hear me? I'm fucking done. This is the last time I will ever see your face. You don't look for me. You don't ask about me. I don't exist to you or anyone like you anymore."

"You need me."

"I don't need shit. I got what I wanted."

"So what? You're going to give it all up for nineteen-year-old pussy?"

I pistol-whipped him, holding him up again.

"If you ever come near me, her, or my family, I swear to God, I'll kill you and anyone who matters to you. I don't care what wars I start. You know what I'm capable of. Fuck around and find out. Do you understand me? Am I making myself crystal fucking clear?"

"You'll be back. They always come back."

I let him go and he crumpled to the ground.

"That's where you're wrong. I have everything I ever wanted now. I've been wanting to be done with you, and the stunt you pulled today fucking proved it." I kicked him in the stomach. "I don't need to kill you to hurt you, William. Me walking away is enough."

With that, I turned and left.

As much as I wanted to put a bullet in his head, death was too good for him. Instead, I walked out there confidently knowing this part of my life was over and now I could focus on a future I didn't think I could have.

All because of my...

Perfect Enemy.

CHAPTER 31
JACE

The following morning, Haven shouted, "Jace!" running down the parking lot to the hospital entrance, where I was waiting for her and my father.

I wasn't surprised that Hayes was with her too.

She jumped into my arms, and I hugged her close to my chest.

"Has Cove woken up yet?"

I pulled away, shaking my head.

"What are the doctors saying?"

"Soon." I hugged my dad and shook Hayes's hand.

"But she's going to be okay, right?"

"She's going to be fine."

"Oh my God, Jace. How did you find her so quickly?"

"Come on. Let's go to Cove's room, so you can see her."

As soon as Haven saw her, she burst into tears. I appreciated that Hayes was there for her. I didn't have it in me to comfort anyone else right now. The staff was kind enough to move Cove to a bigger, private room with a couch I could sleep on, so I spent the night at the hospital. I went back to the safe house to wash up and change my clothes, but I wasn't there for very long.

I needed to get back to my girl.

After Haven had a minor meltdown, she asked me again, "How did you find her?"

I eyed Hayes, and he quickly caught on.

"I'm going to head to the cafeteria and get you guys some coffee." He kissed Haven's head and left, closing the door behind him.

Dad coaxed, "You're scaring me, Jace. What's going on?"

"You both need to sit down."

They did in the chairs right in front of me.

"I don't know how to say this, so I'm just going to come out and say it. For the last ten years, I've done a lot of things I'm not proud of."

"Like in the Navy?" Haven asked.

"No."

"I don't understand."

"To make a really long story short, I lost a really close friend of mine, and it was right after Mom died. I was lost and one thing led to another, and a couple of months later, I lost someone else who mattered a lot to me. They both died in my arms."

Haven breathed out, "Oh my God. Why didn't you ever say anything?"

"I don't know. Now looking at it from another perspective, I wish I would have."

Dad asked, "What were you involved in, Jace?"

"It doesn't matter. I'm not in it anymore, and I've wanted to get out for a while."

"What does Cove have to do with this?"

"There are a lot of blanks I can't fill in for either of you. Just know that Cove is safe now and so am I."

They looked at each other for a second.

"I love you both very much. Please know that I wouldn't ever put your life in danger."

"Does Cove know what happened?"

"Somewhat."

"Does she know who took her?" Haven pleaded with her eyes. "Can we find them?"

I sighed, sharing, "I took her."

They jerked back, caught off guard.

"I was trying to keep her safe."

"Jace, none of this makes any sense."

"I know, Dad. Please… I just need you to trust me when I say it's over. I promise."

Haven shrugged. "So what happens next?"

I didn't hesitate in responding, "She's coming home with me."

"Wait?" Haven paused. "What?"

"You heard me."

"Why would she come home with you?"

I could see it in her eyes. Everything Cove said about my sister and us being together was right. Haven wanted this between Cove and me. It was written all over her face.

I gave her the only honesty I could, replying, "I'm in love with Cove."

Cove

Did I just imagine Jace saying he loved me?

No. My eyes were open.

Was I hallucinating?

As if he felt me from across the room, Jace's stare connected with mine. He smiled before exclaiming, "She's awake."

Haven immediately turned around, hauling ass over to me. She carefully grabbed my hand and kissed it.

"I'm so happy to see you, Cove."

The beeping sound of the heart monitor shifted my attention to the machines on the left side of my body. The rhythmic hissing sound of the ventilator echoed all around me.

I immediately felt panicked, but my mouth was too dry to talk. Jace quickly walked out of the room, and I almost fell into a fit of tears that he was suddenly gone.

What's going on? Why am I in the hospital?

Haven must have read my rattled expression. "You're okay," she insisted, gripping my hand a little harder.

Seconds later, a nurse hurried into the room with Jace behind her. The instant relief I felt that he was back in my space comforted me and lessened the shock of waking up in a hospital room with machines hooked up to my body.

"Welcome back, Cove," she greeted with a gentle smile.

She shined lights in my eyes, took my vitals, and grabbed me a cup of ice water with a straw to wet my throat so I could speak. After she began asking me question after question of what I remembered or what I didn't, and how I felt, she ended her protocols and finally left me alone with my family and Jace. It felt like she went on forever.

Haven grabbed my hand again. "I was so worried I'd never see you again."

"I was with your brother. I was always safe."

"Yeah… that's what he said."

I wanted to talk to Jace, but I knew Haven was dying to hear everything. I didn't want to send him away. However, my best friend was just as important to me.

"Can you guys give us a minute?"

"I'm glad you're okay, Cove." Her dad kissed my head. "You gave us quite a scare."

"Thank you, Mr. Beckham."

He lovingly smiled at me, whispering in my ear, "I have a feeling you're not going to be calling me that very soon."

We looked at each other for a moment. I guess that was his blessing…

Once they were gone, she shut the door behind them.

Haven instantly ordered, "Spill. Everything."

For the next twenty minutes, I caught her up on all of what happened between us.

"Oh my God! You gave your virginity to Jace!"

"Shhh!"

Her hands flew to her mouth. "I knew it!"

"Haven, they're going to hear you."

"I told you. I freaking knew it."

"Yeah, you did. You're a psychic."

"There was way too much passion between the two of you when he carried you out of the bar and then he started calling you bunny. It was so obvious you two were into one another."

I shrugged, confessing, "I've actually had a crush on him since I was eight."

Her mouth dropped open. "What?"

"I know… don't be mad. I should have told you, but back then, I thought you'd be upset, and he was twenty years older than me so nothing could ever come of it when I was that young. Things are different now."

She shook her head, smiling. "I can't believe it. This is just crazy but amazing at the same time."

"You're not mad?"

"I mean, I'm upset you never told me any of this." She smirked. "But I'm way too excited not to forgive you."

"Gee, thanks."

She squealed. "Do you think you'll get married?"

"I think you're jumping way ahead. I can barely get him to say he likes me."

"Well, he just told us he loves you and you're going home with him."

My eyes widened. "I didn't imagine that?"

She beamed, standing from the chair she was sitting on beside my bed. "I'm going to start planning your wedding, so you need to get better."

"Haven—"

"What? He's pushing forty. He's not getting any younger."

My heart fluttered.

"Maybe we can get pregnant at the same time!"

"You need to slow your roll. Besides, I thought you wanted to finish college before you got married and knocked up?"

"Interesting." She wiggled her eyebrows. "You mention me and not yourself?"

I blushed.

"Ahhh! We're going to be sisters!"

"Haven, stop screaming."

"I can't help it. I'm too excited."

"You're jumping way ahead of yourself."

"Again, you're a spring chicken. Jace is going to want to lock you down. He's always been very possessive of his things, and you won't be any different."

I changed the subject. "Have you talked to my parents?"

"My dad has."

"Are they coming to see me?"

She frowned. "I'm sorry, Cove."

"Yeah…" I retorted.

Grabbing my hand again, she sat down. "They don't matter anymore. You've always been a part of my family, and now Jace is going to make it official."

I contemplated what she was stating with such certainty. For as long as I could remember, I wanted to have my parents. For the first time in my life, it didn't feel like I needed them.

Because I was silently hoping…

Haven was right.

CHAPTER 32
JACE

I pulled the chair closer to her beautiful face. Reaching for her hand next, I lifted it to my mouth and kissed her palm.

"Don't ever die on me again."

"I still can't believe that happened."

"Were you being honest with the nurse? Do you really not remember what happened?"

"Everything after telling you I hated you in the garden is gone. I don't remember being shot, Jace, and I'm kind of grateful for that. I don't want to remember it."

I nodded.

"Can you fill in some blanks for me, though?"

I nodded again.

"Who was it? Do you know who shot me?"

"I do."

"Okay…"

"I took care of it."

"That's all I get?"

"Bunny, you're safe. That's all you need to know."

"Alright." She moped for a second. "What about you?"

"I'm safe too."

"And your family?"

I kissed her hand again. "You don't have to worry about anything. I took care of it all."

"What does that mean?"

"It means, I'm finally free."

Her eyebrows pinched together. "How free?"

"Since you don't remember being shot, I imagine you don't remember anything after that either."

She shook her head.

"Well, that part I can fill you in on." Inhaling a deep breath, I prepared myself for what I had to tell her. "I'm not going to sugarcoat it for you, bunny."

"I'd expect nothing less. You don't have much of a bedside manner, but I still want to know."

"You died, Cove."

She slightly gasped.

"It was the scariest fucking minute of my life."

Her lips parted. "I don't know what to say. How did I—"

"I performed CRP and shocked you myself."

She frowned. "I don't understand."

"The paramedic called your death and I just reacted. I fought for you and thank God I did."

"Holy shit, you saved my life."

"I wouldn't have been able to make it without you. I couldn't lose you, bunny."

"Do you mean that?"

"With every bone in my body."

Even with all her swollen face, she was still fucking beautiful. I wanted to reach up and place a strand of hair behind her ear and kiss each imperfection that marred her flawless skin. Instead, I sat back and admired her from afar. Her eyes were so full of life, gazing back at me like I was everything to her.

"You wanted to know the pieces to my puzzle, and I told you. Do you remember what happened before getting shot?"

She bowed her head, letting me know she did.

"I'm sorry you had to go through that twice, Jace. I can only imagine what it felt like for you, especially since you lost Hope and her baby. Losing someone you love is always hard, no matter the circumstances."

Not hesitating, I expressed, "I wasn't in love with her. She was never mine, bunny. Our bond simply came from losing Tony. She was always in love with him. Even in her letters I saw how much she still wanted to be with him. We were just two lost souls who found each other, and it was comforting to feel like I had someone who understand what I was going through. Hope was easy to talk to because I was writing her letters. Almost as if I was writing in a journal. Nothing of what I shared with her was ever face-to-face. Do you understand what I'm saying?"

"I do. It sucks to feel alone."

"You're not alone. You have Haven, my family, and most of all, you have me. You'll always have me."

"What do you mean I have you?"

Brushing the hair away from her cheek, I let my fingers linger and peered deep into her eyes. "I love you, Cove Noel."

Her smile lit up her entire face.

"I told you I loved you when you were dying in my arms, and I'll say it over and over again if that's what it takes to keep you in my life."

Tears filled her gaze.

"Please don't cry."

"They're happy tears."

Unable to resist, I leaned forward and kissed them away as they slid down her cheeks. "I'm so fucking in love with you. You're the first woman I've ever been in love with, bunny. I promise that I'll never hurt you again."

"I love you too," she cried, wrapping her arms around my neck.

"You're the best thing that's ever happened to me."

She shut her eyes, going through the motions of what I was confessing. I kissed my way to her mouth, needing to taste heaven again. When her heart rate accelerated on her monitor, I reluctantly pulled away.

"They're going to kick me out if we don't stop."

She giggled. "When do I get to leave?"

Once again, I didn't waver. "As soon as you're discharged, you're moving in with me."

Cove

I grinned, teasing, "I don't remember you asking."

"I'm not asking, I'm telling you."

"What if I say no?"

"I'll have to kidnap you again."

"You can kidnap me anytime you want."

I was caught off guard when he added, "I have something for you."

"What?"

It was only then I noticed there was something sticking out of his pocket. There in front of my glossy stare was a stuffed animal I never thought I'd see.

My mouth dropped open.

"You have my bunny?"

"I've had it since you gave it to me. It's traveled all over the world with me."

My heart was breaking in the best way possible as he handed it to me.

"I was so fucking drunk that night you followed me out to the stream. It was after my mom's funeral, and I couldn't take one more person giving me their condolences. I was so angry, I just started drinking. It was the only thing that numbed the pain."

"I understand. I shouldn't have—"

"No, bunny. I shouldn't have treated you like that. I barely remember any of it until you called me out on it in the garden. I'm so fucking sorry I treated you that way. I would never have if I'd been sober. I took my frustration out on the wrong person and if I could go back, I'd change everything about your kind gesture."

"How much of it do you remember?"

"Enough that I went back there the next morning and saw your bunny on the ground. I should have given it back to you, but for some reason, it gave me comfort in a moment where I needed all I could get. In a way, you've been by my side ever since."

I smiled, loving the effect I had on him.

"Why didn't you ever bring it up?"

I shrugged. "I don't know. I was embarrassed, and the guy I had the biggest crush on just broke my heart. It's why I hated you so much."

He nodded. "It all makes sense." I could see it in her eyes. "Ask me, Cove."

"Is that why you call me bunny?"

"Mm-hmm."

"Ah. And your feelings for me… how long have you had them?"

He grinned, leaning back into the chair. "I knew you were going to ask me that."

"Well, you are G.I. Joe after all."

"Let me lay it out for you, bunny. That night at the bar, I could have killed that motherfucker just because he was dancing with you."

"So you were jealous?"

"Not as much as I was when I walked in on you and Deacon."

"I knew it."

"I always tortured my enemies for information before anything else. Deacon was the first man I killed point blank without finding out a single thing. From the second I saw him on top of you, I fucking lost it. I wasn't planning on ending him that fast or doing it in front of you, but the mere sight of you about to give your cherry was too real. I acted on pure impulse and fucking killed him just for you."

"Wow," I breathed out. "I was not expecting you to say that."

He leaned forward on his elbows. "Get used to it. I'm going to be full of surprises when it comes to you."

"I'm looking forward to it."

"For the first time in my life"—he kissed me—"I'm looking forward to my future with you."

"I love you, Jace."

"I fucking love you, Cove."

I always knew…

The villain would turn out to be my hero.

CHAPTER 33
COVE
ONE YEAR LATER

Words couldn't describe the last twelve months of my life. They were the best, and I knew it was from Jace being in my life. We spent all our time together. Since he was retired, he didn't have a job to report to, and all I had was college classes. The moments in between, we were together doing normal things like any couple.

His family was everything to me. Haven was thrilled that we were in a relationship. I'd never seen her so happy before with Hayes in her life and Jace and I together. Everything between us just felt right.

I hadn't seen my parents since I left the hospital. Not even when I went home and packed up my things with Jace. They never reached out, trying to see me, but it didn't matter. I never needed them. They could have each other.

After living in Jace's condo, we decided we wanted to own something together instead. We spent months finding our perfect home.

"Now what?" I baited, spreading my legs on the stairs of our house.

We just closed on our thirty-five-hundred square foot, four bedroom, four bath home with an office home that afternoon. Now I only had one thing on my mind.

"I have something in mind."

"Me too." I arched an eyebrow. "Get on your knees, soldier."

He didn't have to be told twice. In a moment's notice, he stripped me naked. When I felt his tongue on my pussy it was warm, wet, soft, and I moaned in arousal. He pushed his tongue as far as it would go into the opening of my core, causing my back to arch and my head to spin.

I rocked my hips against his mouth, and he slid his lips up to my clit.

"Yes," I panted, thinking I was going to pass out from the desire of feeling him this way.

Jace was extremely talented in everything he did, but when it came down to me, he was a skilled expert on my body. He sucked on my clit, up and down and side to side, humming. It made it that much more intense for me. He was always about my pleasure, no matter what, I always came first.

"Please don't stop, please keep doing that," I shamelessly begged.

He reached up and cupped my breasts, rubbing and teasing my nipples. I couldn't take it anymore and once he grabbed my hips to move them faster and harder, I started to shake, and my vision began to blur. The room became hot, and I couldn't help the noises coming out of my mouth.

I finally felt myself come apart, and I came so hard that my head fell back against one of the steps. He instantly kissed me, and I tasted myself. Which only added to my desire of wanting his cock inside me.

We kissed, devouring each other's mouths, trying to capture every feeling, every taste that lingered between us. Lifting me up, he sat down before he turned me around with my back to his front.

He bit my shoulder.

"Ow! What was that for?"

Softly, he kissed the bite mark, not saying a word, and placed a few more kisses along my shoulder blades. Then he bit me again.

"Ow! What are you doing?" I tried moving away, but he held me firmer.

I could feel him smiling, though he still didn't say anything. He repeated the process a few more times, leaving bite marks from one shoulder to the other and then tenderly kissed every last one, trailing kisses back up to my ear.

"My bunny."

I smiled, nodding.

"You know what I want?"

"Hmmm…"

"I'm going to fuck you on these stairs."

I looked back at him, and he kissed along my jawline.

"Tell me, Cove. Where are you right now?" he questioned with a certain edge in his tone.

"I'm on your cock, ready for you to fuck me senseless."

"Where else are you?"

I gazed back at him, knowing what he wanted. "Home."

I rocked my hips on his hard dick as he jerked my head back by my hair, making me moan in response. Resting my hands on his thighs, I opened my legs further. He took my silent plea and his fingers crept to my clit.

"You're so fucking wet for me," he groaned into my neck.

He used his palm and fingers to manipulate my clit, and I moved my hips in the opposite direction that he stimulated. My clit was overly exposed from this angle, and it didn't take long for my wetness to pool again.

"That feel good?"

There was something animalistic in his voice that I loved. I sucked in my lower lip, and he let up on my hair, shifting to grab the back of my neck instead. His fingers quickly slipped into my opening, and my head wanted to fall back his shoulder. He held me firm in place, where he could watch my face come apart while he finger fucked my G-spot like a man a mission.

My mouth parted.

My breathing escalated.

My eyes started rolling to the back of my head.

As I was about to come, he ordered, "Pull out my cock."

After I did, he sat me on his dick before I even saw it coming, and he roughly thrusted deep inside me.

I came on the spot.

My body trembled and my come dripped down his balls. He didn't give me any time to recover as he turned our bodies to stand and grab the stair railing.

"Lean forward," he huskily ordered.

I did as I was told, and he gripped my hips.

Hard.

I knew there would be markings all over my body when he finished having his way with me, and I fucking loved it. Gripping my hair by the nape of my neck, he yanked it back again. He was basically fucking me doggy style, except we were standing.

"Fuck… your pussy was made for me."

He pulled out his dick, causing me to whimper at the loss, but he quickly grabbed my leg, and placed it on the railing. I began shaking from the awkward angle.

"I got you, you're not going to fall," he stated, reading my body.

I nodded and in one deep thrust he was back inside me, slamming in and out of me. My noises grew louder and louder the closer I got to release. He fucked me harder and faster, mercilessly pounding into me.

Jace and I were so perfect together. I didn't like soft or gentle, I loved it when he fucked me like this. It always felt like he was marking and claiming me in such a primal way.

"That's it… squeeze my cock with your tight pussy that I can't get enough of…"

The slapping sound of our skin-on-skin contact echoed in the room.

"Yes…yes…yes…" I screamed out.

My body shuddered, and I almost lost my balance from my intense and overpowering orgasm. However, Jace kept me upright. I tried to keep his pace, barely done with one release when another would hit.

"I fucking love you," he growled from deep within his chest.

I fell forward, clenching onto his cock, and he made this roaring sound as we came together.

We both panted profusely, trying to catch our bearings, and he kissed all over my face, not removing himself from inside me.

"Welcome home, Cove."

And he had just fucked me, meaning every last word of it.

I couldn't have been happier, and it had everything to do with the man I was madly in love with.

Jace

After we showered together, I threw on a pair of gym shorts as he lay on the mattress on the floor.

"I can't wait for all our new furniture to come in tomorrow!"

"I know, you've been telling me all day."

"I think I want to wallpaper this back wall where our bed will be."

"Whatever you want."

"What color do you think?"

"I don't care. Whatever you want."

"Jace, do you want blue or turquoise or maybe even lavender?"

"Bunny, whatever makes you happy."

"Fine. How about pink?"

"No pink."

I giggled.

"You can save that for our baby girl's room."

"Little girl, huh? That's not how it works. You know, first comes marriage, then comes baby, so we're missing a step."

I smiled.

"Why are you looking at me like that?"

In three strides, I was sitting on the edge of the mattress and holding out a ring box. There was no doubt in my mind that she was mine forever. The past year of our lives was truly the best time of my life. I couldn't believe my soulmate had been my little sister's best friend this entire time. Simply proving that we were meant to be together.

There was no reason to wait any longer.

No more enemies.

No more demons.

Just her.

Always Cove.

I didn't give her a chance to reply before my mouth was on hers, kissing her gently and adoringly.

I savored every touch.

Every push and pull.

Every movement of my lips working against hers.

It was one giant buildup of months of me wanting this moment between us. I kissed her deeper, harder, and with more determination. The passion that radiated off her, stirring spasms down my body. I lay her back on the bed, hovering above as I grabbed her hand.

I never stopped claiming her mouth as I slid the diamond down her ring finger.

"I love you," I rasped between kisses.

"I love you, too," she murmured, not breaking our connection. "I want you."

"You have me," I groaned. "You've always fucking had me." Setting my forehead on hers, I peered deep into her eyes. "Marry me."

She beamed.

"I—"

"I'm not asking. I'm telling you."

She laughed, throwing her arms around my neck. "I love you! I love you! I love you!" Extending her hand from behind me, she shouted, "Oh my God! It's huge!"

I knew she was talking about her ring, but I still stated, "There's nothing little about me."

She giggled, kissing my neck.

I spent the rest of the night making love to her.

As my future wife.

EPILOGUE
COVE
THREE MONTHS LATER

"**Y**ou need to stop," I chastised as Jace backed me into his old bedroom at his dad's house.

"You know that's only going to make me keep going."

I murmured, "Your entire family and friends are downstairs. We cannot have sex right now."

"Why are you whispering?" He shut the door behind him.

"I don't know." Smirking, I decided to push his buttons. "It's a force of habit when guys sneak me into their bedrooms."

He cocked his head to the side, grinning. "You blinked."

"Shit! I really need to learn how to be a better liar."

"You're going to pay for that one."

"Jace, don't you dar—"

He tackled me to his bed, and I loudly shrieked, giggling at the same time.

"I don't know how I should punish you." He hovered above me, caging me in with his arms around my face. "With my cock in your pussy or your ass?"

I wiggled my eyebrows. He'd claimed all of my holes. "That doesn't sound like much punishment to me."

"I didn't say I'd let you come."

I pouted. "That's super rude."

"Bad girls don't get to come, bunny."

I kissed him. "But you love it when I'm a very bad girl."

"That's only when you're riding my cock."

"You're horrible."

"You love it."

I smiled, rubbing my lips against his. "Your dad will kill us if we don't go downstairs and mingle with everyone."

"I'm not worried about it. All my brothers are down there and so is Haven with whatever his name is."

"Jace... you know his name is Hayes."

Although Haven was madly in love with Hayes, and they were pretty much engaged too, Jace still busted his balls. He was forever the role of the oldest protective brother.

"I hope our son is just like you with his little sister."

"You weren't saying that last year."

"That's because I wanted to fight with you to get your attention."

"You were just pretending to be my perfect enemy?"

I sang, "Not as much as you were."

He bit my neck.

I chuckled, shrugging my shoulder, trying to get him out of there.

"Come on, we need to go."

He groaned.

"Your brothers want to see you. Alexander is only in town for the weekend, he has a new movie he starts next week."

His brothers never questioned Jace on what he did, but they knew he was out of that life. They were happy to have him around again. Since he left for the military at eighteen, he had a lot of years to make up for.

"I can't wait for you to be Mrs. Beckham."

"I can't wait to be Mrs. Beckham."

We were getting married in the fall, and I couldn't wait. I finally had everything I ever wanted, and it only took being kidnapped to make that happen. The irony was not lost on me.

However, Jace said we would always have ended up together.

Jace

Giving in to my persistent sexual needs, she coaxed, "You can have your way with me, but you have to be quick."

My hand slid down her stomach only to be interrupted by a knock on the door.

"We're busy!" I shouted.

"No, we're not!"

"You may want to come downstairs," Haven stressed.

I muttered, "I want to come alright..."

Cove slapped my chest, pushing me up, and I unwillingly gave in.

I'd take my time with her later. Every day was better than the last with her by my side. I couldn't have been happier with how things turned out between us. She meant everything to me.

"Come in, Haven," I announced.

She did, and from the expression on her face, this couldn't be good.

"What's going on?"

"Ummm... I'm not really sure. Just come downstairs."

I grabbed Cove's hand, following Haven out of the room. I'd be lying if I said I wasn't nervous with each step I took until Ledger came into view.

"Why are you here, Hazel? What else do you need from our ranch that you haven't already tried to take?"

Only then did I notice our family's biggest competitor standing in front of him.

"We need to talk."

"Whatever you need to say, you can do it in front of my family."

Reading people was what I excelled at, and what she was about to announce was going to shock the shit out of us.

"Fine! Have it your way."

I couldn't have been more right.

When she declared...

"I'm pregnant with your baby!"

The end

For Jace and Cove.

*It's only the beginning, or is it also **the end** for…*
Ledger and Hazel

SINFUL ENEMY

(Standalone/Enemies to Lovers Romance)
Releasing July 25, 2023

PRE-ORDER AVAILABLE NOW

From Wall Street Journal and USA Today Bestselling Author M. Robinson comes an enemies to lovers, surprise baby, standalone romance.

If I knew what was good for me, I would've stayed away.
But then again, I've never been much for following the rules.
She was all work and no play and an enemy to my father's ranch—
making her an enemy to me and my legacy.
A drunken one-night stand with Ms. Polished Perfection seemed like a
good way to pass the time in the city.
Now I can't stay away from her. Not just because she's the only thing
standing between the ranch and its ruination, but because she just
showed up on my front door six weeks later…
Pregnant with my baby.

SECOND CHANCE SERIES

Second Chance Contract
Second Chance Vow
Second Chance Scandal
Second Chance Love
Second Chance Rival
Second Chance Mine

Other Series to Check Out:

ANGSTY ROM-COM
The Kiss
The Fling

MAFIA/ORGANIZED CRIME ROMANCE
El Diablo
El Santo
El Pecador
Sinful Arrangement
Mafia Casanova: Co-written with Rachel Van Dyken
Falling for the Villain: Co-written with Rachel Van Dyken

SMALL TOWN ROMANCE
Complicate Me
Forbid Me
Undo Me
Crave Me

EROTIC ROMANCE

VIP

The Madam

MVP

Two Sides

Tempting Bad

MEET M. ROBINSON

M. Robinson is the Wall Street Journal and USA Today Bestselling author of more than thirty novels in Contemporary Romance and Romantic Suspense. Crowned the "Queen of Angst" by her loyal readers, you'll feel the cut of her pen slicing through your heart as your soul bleeds upon the words of her stories with each turn of the page. Most notably known for the Good Ol' Boys, M's newest venture has graced her with the #1 Bestseller on Apple Books with Second Chance Contract. The Second Chance Men are powerful, intelligent and will sweep you off your feet and leave you weak in the knees—every woman's wildest dreams.

M. lives the boat life along the Gulf Coast of Florida with her two puppies and real life book boyfriend, the inspiration for all her filthy talking alphas, Bossman.

When she isn't in the cave writing her next epic love story, you can usually spot her mad-dashing through Target or in the drive-thru of Starbucks, refueling. Yes, she's a self-proclaimed shopaholic, but only if she's spending Bossman's money.

You can follow M, Ted, Marley, and Bossman on Facebook, Instagram, and her absolute favorite social platform-TikTok.

www.authormrobinson.com

ACKNOWLEDGMENTS

Personal Assistant: Renee Mccleary
Cover Designer: Lori Jackson
Paperback Formatter: Sarah Barton
Ebook Formatter: Leanne Trn
Publicist: Danielle Sanchez
Agent: Stephanie DeLamater Phillips

Bloggers/Bookstagrammers: Without you I'd be nothing. Thank you for all your support always.

My VIPS/Readers

Photographer: Wander Aguilar
Model: James Ransom

Street Team Leaders: Leeann Van Rensburg & Jamie Guellar
Teasers & Promo: Shereads.pang, Leanne Trn, Madaline Bird

My VIP Reader Group Admins:
Lily Garcia, Leeann Van Rensburg, Jennifer Pon, Jessica Laws, Louisa Brandenburger

Street Team & Hype Girls: You're the best.

My alphas & betas:
Thank you for helping me bring this book to life.

Made in the USA
Columbia, SC
28 February 2025

54534402R00135